Playing House

To Richard
& Paula
whom I love
more than any
others

Rita

Playing House

———◆———

Fredrica Wagman

HOLT, RINEHART AND WINSTON

New York   Chicago   San Francisco

Grateful acknowledgment is made
to Warner Bros. Music for permission to quote from
"Mr. Tambourine Man" by Bob Dylan, © 1965 M. Witmark & Sons.
All rights reserved.
Used by permission of Warner Bros. Music.
Portions of the song appear on pages 127 and 151.

Published simultaneously in Canada by Holt, Rinehart
and Winston of Canada, Limited.
Library of Congress Cataloging in Publication Data
Wagman, Fredrica.
Playing house.
I. Title.
PZ4.W1315Pl [PS3573.A36] 813'.5'4 72-93181
ISBN 0-03-007746-X
FIRST EDITION
Printed in the United States of America

To Philip Roth

PART I

I

Can't concentrate. My mind is wandering over him crouched on top of me, over his shoulders to a summer day again, always back to then when a room was filled with sun gold, when the walls were white, when the window glass was crystal clear and there was sunshine always dancing on the floor. Heavy brown silk rugs made a border all around the bed where he pinned me there and said that if I told he'd beat me with the branches of the tree and I never told, no matter what he did I never told, he was my brother.

How old were we then? I can't remember, very young, just children, just his laughing mouth, just his straight blond hair and always the blue shirt. His face was soft, puffy, almost as if there were no bones in it at all, not even all his urgency could put bones back into his face, red cheeks, country hands, peasant hands that were flat and thick, his nails bitten down to nothing.

He was the master, I was the slave who kept the steady beat, that was the game we played that put the urgency into his face and though I didn't know what we were after, I went with him. I kept going with him until it happened, until he made it happen rocking on top of me, pinning me under him, keeping me, pressing himself against me hard, on and on, weary and exhausted I kept going with him until it broke loose all over me and swallowed me up into it.

That first enormous thing of ecstasy, yes, then, so long ago. And the monumental shock of it, the bewildering incomparable immediate acceptance of it, the sudden understanding of what the secret is tumbling out of all the little hiding places in my body, this hint we're born with suddenly broke loose with him crouching over me, pinning me with the sunshine and the gleaming walls and the sparkling window glass—and him.

The soft bedsheets of childhood suddenly yielded up a different meaning, a different message in their dishevelment. Now a bed became some brand-new thing, pillows that were dented where heads sunk into them said something. "Don't tell," they said. "You must never tell about this thing. Hide it away, smooth away the evidence. It's the Secret."

Never tell, never tell. We never said a word about it, not to anyone, not to each other and I thought then that something happened that no one else on earth had ever known, no one else on earth had ever fathomed or imagined and I knew that it was something that was forbidden. It was a secret monumental accident, but a forbidden accident. That by some strange stroke of driving luck we hit upon the secret of the universe and we were the only people who ever had. I thought then in some childish, illogical way that we were supreme freaks, twisted, wicked, naughty, vile creatures who lucked out on some gigantic mistake no one ever allowed us to have the slightest understanding of, not in any way, no hint, no indications ever.

This amazing thing had been kept from us, protected by stern faces and silences, protected by warnings of going blind or madness maybe if we dared to touch, never touch, never go near there, bad girl, bad, bad girl. Stern hands pulling our wandering fingers away from the very first.

With scrupulous care we were made to believe that human beings merely walked or ran or hurt or ate or cried or did their jobs and waited, not discovered. They kept the real secret from us as best they could and yet we triumphed into all of it despite them, and it was ours.

Uncomplicated then, it seemed so uncomplicated that first time. So huge and simple, so overwhelming, like gratitude or hunger, it had no shadows, no veils, it was the product of integrity, of wholeness. I was a total person then, caught up into a total happening. Children we were, twins I used to think, more than twins, one person, my brother and I, separate from the rest of them, removed from them, outside the world, shameful, wicked, bad, lucky freaks we were, my brother and I.

I keep trying to remember on a little greedy inventory register how many times, exactly how many times like that, graphic times, the rainstorm times, the spring or winter, maybe summer times, how many? It's hard to say how many times, a lot of times that all melt into the memory of him, just him in a wordless tacit understanding about a secret that was ours. And then one day he was gone.

His bedroom empty, the bed was made and everything in there was left in perfect order with a stillness that was death.

I looked everywhere for him but he was gone. He went away. Boarding school my mother said. Boarding school. My mind held on to him as the rest of the world crashed into blackness all around me, something like how it must feel to be drowning in the ocean in the dead of night, hanging on to a phantom, trying to survive. "Endure," this one voice in my head kept saying, "just somehow endure."

I drifted out there lost a long, long time. A vague childhood after that of wandering and waiting, feeling seasons joylessly, receiving vague impressions, losing vague images, arriving for moments at imaginativeness and renewal and then losing this again to the one-dimensional and empty days living had become after he went away.

Homesickness became the only feeling I possessed, the nameless longing, the grieving, the counting days and hours and days again, the waiting mingling with wispy hope in some far-off distant way. What was I hoping for? I almost forgot. What was I waiting for, I couldn't say exactly. Something, something. A reunion maybe, a dream, a fantasy? I didn't know. It all had gone so far away from me, pain shrouded my brother's face so that I could hardly see him anymore, until loss and my brother became one thing inseparable, when reunion finally lured me and with it the search began. A search that was never satisfied, a search that was always intertwined with homesickness, the overwhelming meaning of my life became a wordless waiting, a search, and suddenly I looked around and my body was big, my feet didn't fit in the same size shoe anymore, the rooms I lived in were all different now, changed, this place is my home, isn't it? Yes. And yet I'm homesick.

This place that smells of feet and cigarettes and newspapers on the floor with a suffocating strangling closeness and it's all still dark, still vague, still one-dimensional and empty with homesickness destroying me.

Little crumbs are in the sheets, funny curtains on the windows over there with the night coming in, in blocks that change and shift and relocate across the ceiling. There's a dark green chair with all the cotton stuffing coming out, tired, weary, going fat and sloppy like an old army general still somehow at attention. The rug around the bed is blue now with crappy *lanterns* in the corners and in the center a nightingale is in a cage, a secondhand nightingale from a secondhand store, tired like all of it has gotten tired with nothing to take its place. The room that has no language anymore like voices without sound, food without taste, sleep without dreams, no dreams, no meaning, this man sleeping next to me, not crouching on me anymore, not suffocating me with his bodyweight, not burdening me any more, has taken all the meaning with him, fucking, fucking until he finished and dropped over, done, to sleep, snoring out the hours and the distance and the strangeness lying there. Who is he? I have no idea. Your husband, that's who he is. Yes of course, my husband, that's right. Can he save me? No, I don't think so, much as he'd like to, it's all too late. He goes too fast, much too fast, he isn't real, like the room isn't real. Real was a train going down the track that went too fast, that's all but lost from sight. Wait, I shout at it, don't go so fast, wait for me for just another minute, another minute might be all I'd need, but it doesn't wait, it's gone. Just the smoke floating on a summer afternoon again. Alone, so utterly alone and flailing, reaching for a cigarette alone, flailing, reaching, grabbing for the smoke, hanging on to phantoms to survive.

I swirled round and round, the pink silk skirt would fly away from me, my petticoats were showing while I twirled. Weren't they remarkable all trimmed in lace, all starchy crinoline, dancing round and round out on the velvet afternoon? Look at me, I'm pretty, really, aren't I? My hair is black, my legs are long and straight, my skirts are flying round and round, I have a little satin sash tied in a bow around my waist, my body is still a tube, my arms are reaching up to touch the clouds.

Warm days rolling out of winter, spring again bursting out of eggshells tearing the thin stuff and filling the world with yellow. The sky hangs so close you can almost touch it with your fingertips, go ahead and touch it, it's close enough today, don't be afraid, fling yourself, no coats, not anymore, open your arms and spread your fingers wide and spin and spin and spin, school's done, there isn't school, not anymore, the crocus peeps up timid, the tulips are bellowing out in belching reds, all the goodness there ever was is here, right here, today, and I'm spinning, filling up the world with warmth again, hold it all before it's gone away, before it shrivels up like shadows and is gone.

"Where were you?" she said. "Where did you go? I've been looking for you for over an hour."

"I was here," I answered her. "Just here."

Her yellow eyes would look at me without a sense of seeing, like a blind person who has trained her lifeless lights to stop where the noise is coming from.

"I was just spinning in my perfect dress, feeling my skirts fly away from me, spinning round and round. I was only here."

"Where's your brother?" she asked me. "Where did he go?"

"I don't know," I answered her. "He's gone but he'll be back."

My mother clutched the shawl around her and went in. Walked across the wooden porch and I heard the click click of her high-heeled slippers, I heard the screen door bang her in, and in my mind I continued watching her, continued watching what she meant, trying to read what she didn't say, tried to look past her question to what she was really thinking. What was she really thinking?

The swan was young then, she didn't come when I held my hand out to her, she didn't notice me, she drifted in the stream beside the house, remote and beautiful, and I watched her and I envied her how much she didn't need. I needed, enormously. I needed everything and suddenly I was aware of myself as hungry, as starving, and I spun around again to see only the closed screen door and no one there. What was my mother thinking?

The house that blinked its eyes, the huge and proud Victorian matriarch pitched across green velvet grass sitting on her haunches. There were porches and pillars and weathervanes, towers and shingles and wrought-iron grills around the roof, every detail was thin and perfect like a tune on a harpsichord at teatime with china cups and saucers and little golden spoons. The great marvelous gingerbread house with bulging bay windows and steeples and shutters all in wood with a wooden porch along the front of her like a double chin. All pretend. So whimsical. The white curtains peeking out of the windows looked like the whites of eyes around the dark black coals that saw everything. The orange house with tan and brown, always pumpkin Halloween-time colors. That house, our house when we were little, where we saw the first of everything, where nothing ever changed, it seemed timeless, stationary against a changing, relocating sky. The seasons never seemed to matter, nothing ever budged in the breeze, it was always the same house with the same dress on, the same hat, the same bustle, a proper, sterile house that would not make allowances. Her house, my mother's house, that never had an odor and not a single blade of grass was ever out of step.

The earth stood still around it, snow never gathered there, the sky always hung in in just the same way every day, the clouds around it never seemed to move, as if the whole thing was painted on the air and everything about it held its breath. There were no shadows, the rain didn't fall on our side of the hedges, only over there, across the property line. The trees were stationed vanguards that had no warmth or humor, just a job to do with crossed arms, no heart left, just principles. About the whole place there was a stillness, a permanency that was rock, that was fixed, immovable, but there was something wailing low, a sense of loss crying out in all the hollowness, in all the gingerbread and properness, in all the sterility there was a sorrow and an aching emptiness. There was no comfort there, no warmth, only a wailing in all the austerity, in all the perched importantness and it would catch me short when I would be dashing in from somewhere, rushing out of breath. Suddenly when I would be inside that house and I could hear it, this chill, silent, empty feeling would devastate me. I would spin around and look at all the shadows, at all the empty hollow rooms and hear it, this thing, this wailing. I would look for it as though I might be able even to see it, as though it had a face.

I would find my brother in the springhouse alone on summer days, always alone, no friends. I never knew what he did when I wasn't with him, what he liked, what he made or cared about. There never seemed to be anything except the waiting, the expressionless waiting, or that urgency. And he frightened me.

In a way he frightened everyone a little, everyone jumped when it came to him, what he liked to eat, how they tried to please him, they smiled at him a lot, they tried to make him laugh. He never made mistakes, no one ever scolded him the way they scolded me. They praised him just by the way they spoke to him. They favored him. When something didn't go his way he went off by himself down to the stream, to the swan. She belonged to him, she came to his hands only, took only his crusts of bread, left everything she was doing when he came and I would follow behind and watch him feeding her and I would watch the swan, remote and knowing, so beautiful, so easy in the water, so in command of herself, like he was, so indifferent. Both my brother and his swan seemed so at ease and in command of everything like they fit in their own skins and even chose the skins they would forever wear.

I was ten that autumn when the apple trees were heavy with their crimson fruit all falling down and he would grab the apples in a sudden outbreak of high spirits and start to throw them at me, laughing, hitting my arms and legs, and I ran away, running up the hill away from him and he kept throwing them and I heard him laughing, laughing, till I couldn't hear him anymore.

"Why are you crying?" I'd hear a voice from the top of the stairs but I never saw the face that said it. I'd never tell her why I cried, I never told a word.

There was a woods behind the school where I used to go, where the sun would come in broad bands of dusty gold like great enormous fingers through the trees. There I'd be able to pause a little bit and hold to myself all the things I was losing. Childhood, sun gold, bits of rocks I'd jam into my pockets and I didn't know then what was going to take their place. I'd stand alone, not wanting to let go of all of it and knowing still, despite my clinging, it was almost gone.

I looked up and saw the shadow of a cat hanging from a tree. I walked closer behind the bushes, creeping terrified up to it to make out the thing I thought I saw, and I saw him there beside it holding a switch in his hand. He didn't see me. The cat was hanging upside down by a rope, blood coming from its nose, my brother standing next to it. The cat was dead.

Later that night I lay in terror in my bed, my mother standing next to me. Yes, I told her what I saw, I had to, not to betray him but to relieve myself of the fear and terror I was suffering. "No," she said. That was all she said. It didn't happen, it was all a mistake, I was wrong.

It was as though I had put something into a drawer and closed it and when I opened the drawer seconds later the thing I put in there was gone.

He was fourteen then, long and thin, blond hair falling straight across his face. He was detached, he drew lines no one ever dared to cross. He drew them with his silences, he drew them with his boredom and his restlessness, with his vague contempt for everything except the swan.

Or else sometimes he broke out into these wild high spirits, sometimes he would come galloping out of his sullenness in a kind of wild different mood completely.

A wall ran along the orchard where the apple trees were growing, a low stone wall. He walked on it, I walked on the grass beside him, my hands trickling along the wall in front of his feet, running the tops of my nails along the ragged stone. He would be telling me stories when suddenly without a word, without an expression on his face, he drove the heel of his shoe into my fingers like he was putting out a cigarette, staring at my face contort in pain. His expression never changed except a little glimmer of a laugh when he released my fingers from his heel.

"No," she'd say, "he wouldn't do a thing like that, you must never tell stories on your brother."

"See," he said, "she'd never believe you anyhow. I'm always right."

His room was at the far end of a sunny hall. There was a bed and a dresser and a desk, shelves for books and little things all over that belonged to him that had a place, that never moved, that he kept in minute and perfect order. I would open the door and find him on the floor cutting things out of magazines and making neat piles of what he cut. I'd find him drawing pictures of unimaginable detail with strange lines and circles, animal faces over monstrous bodies, thousand-legged creatures or grotesque people, pasting words and faces on them from the magazines and he'd tell me to come and look. There were always stories that went with them, stories about beasts and storms and being eaten alive, that somewhere in the house, in this great old scary windy house the creatures lived and waited and if I wasn't very good he'd let them out on me to eat me and devour me, and I ran screaming from his room and then I'd find him standing in the doorway of my room looking at me. How old was I then? Still ten I guess, maybe eleven, I can't remember, I can't say exactly. He was waiting then, standing there, and while he waited, the expression on his face slowly changed to urgency, slipping over him like a stocking over a foot and then the leg. He frightened me and he fascinated me both at once, and I'd remember what it felt like with him. I'd remember the little rippling electric waves rolling over me again and again if he would only climb on top of me and begin to rock, pressing hard against me, pinning me there, holding me down on the floor, on his bed, down in the springhouse. We could hear my mother calling. I'd stir and he'd put his hand over my mouth and crumple over me, gasping and exhausted, till it happened, again, another time, just once more, until he went away.

A little bunch of flowers at my bedroom door, a book with funny pictures in it, a thing of dusting powder, an envelope with seven dollars, one of his sweaters, a camera he brought

12

me from New York, toys, always a little present, no reason. "Come and get it," he would shout, and when I vomited he held my head, and he'd bring me ginger ale, and he'd sit with me until I fell asleep.

"You'll never leave. You'll never go away?"

"No," he used to say and he'd look away.

"Maybe we can get married one day?" I asked him.

"No," he said, pushing the yellow hair off his face, turning away from me, gentle, smiling, soft face that had no bones in it, pink then from the thing we had that happened not completely gone from him. Still flushed. "It doesn't matter," he would answer me, "brothers and sisters can't be married, don't you know, if they do, then their kids have blood diseases, become idiots, it's not important anyhow, it doesn't matter, it never will."

"Don't go," I used to say to him. "Don't ever go." But he only used to turn away and bite his nails.

In my mind it seemed as though he were the one who commanded the sun to rise in the morning and set each night exactly the way he had decided it should. He knew everything. He was the one who invented certain words that everybody used, words like "certainly" and "not particularly." He commanded people just by looking at them or by being silent, and his moods, his shifting shadows, were what the days consisted of, there was no weather, no winter or summer, it was just his moods. He created atmospheres, everybody worried about him, everybody tiptoed around him, around his frowns, he was the center of the universe, all the rest of us made up the borders.

We had a sister who had red hair, who lived alone and talked to herself, who never liked to lend things or let anyone in her room, who cried a lot and finally one day killed herself.

She had the same strange yellow lights my mother had that could focus where the noise was coming from but never saw a thing except her own gray shadows going up the stairs. Sarah. She was the oldest. The train went too fast for her too, she couldn't grab the smoke. Sometimes the train just goes too fast racing along the steely tracks away, over the flat, low, gray-green night through the brownish trees and little canals that grow along the side of railroad tracks, empty tracts of land that border emptiness, an emptiness not touching people, not holding them in your arms and hearing words that can save, wise words, wisdom words, real meaning words. Combing your hair and fixing ribbons in it to make you beautiful, straightening out a skirt and seeing it fall just right, choosing the perfect pair of shoes and smiling in a mirror to see how wonderful the whole thing happens to work out when everything is real, when everything tastes good and makes you warm and comfortable with a little hint of joy lurking in there somewhere, almost breaking loose. It used to be that way when spring would come again breaking out of eggshells, bursting out in yellow lace, in brand-new leaves and velvet grass again, twirling round in my pink silk skirts and feeling them fly away from me out there, reaching up to touch the sky.

But now the train is racing down the tracks too fast. How long have I been living in a fog? How long have I been grabbing after smoke? And far down is the street.

The window is open with the night coming in, the sleeping man is out of reach, sleeping in his satiation, snoring out the emptiness. Who did you say he was? My husband, that's right, my husband.

"Does it run in families?" I turn to him, waking him. "I mean about my sister?"

"No," he says, "how many times do I have to tell you? No."

Why can't I trust him? I'm thinking. Because he's so much a total stranger to me, this husband-stranger-man. I have no anger for him, no contempt, nothing. He doesn't matter, he can't save me, he's here by mistake and if I close my eyes in the morning he'll be gone.

No, he won't be gone, day after day after night after weeks and months and years with your hair getting gray and chins coming out and stomach trouble and trouble walking he won't be gone. He'll still be there sleeping next to you, foreign and inaccessible with nothing to say that helps, that helps getting old and hurting and coming undone or falling apart.

He could never put me back together. If I ask him what time it is, or what day it is or what year, he'll answer me. In the morning he'll wonder if I took my pills but if I ask him if it runs in families—destruction, suicide, yellow eyes that never see but only focus where the noise is coming from—if I ask him why it's all this way, where the road took the crazy twisting detour into woods and brambles, into tangles and rocks with gigantic laughing faces and cats hanging dead beside a stream, or was it in the woods? No, not a swan, a redheaded girl who never liked to lend things, a dead cat, the sun-filled room at the far end of the hall, my mother looking at me.

"Where is he?" she would say, "where did he go?" Where did he go? I asked her. The dead cat, the switch in his hands and Sarah lying on the kitchen floor in a fur coat, dead, twenty-five Nembutals pumped into her, clutching car keys in her hand. Where would she have gone? Where was she headed for when she dropped over holding the car keys? No, he doesn't know the answers with his shoulder hugged around the pillow. My turtle husband hiding in his tortoiseshell around him, he never knew those answers. My Turtle in his shell would only mutter from his sleep, "Not this again."

"Can I have a cigarette?" I ask him sleeping there. "Would you get a cigarette for me? There are more on the table over there but the window's open and far down below is the street and it scares me. I'm afraid to move out of bed and cross the room to get the other pack. I'm afraid of the window, it might eat me up, it might devour me."

"Not this again," he says from his pillow bosom he keeps

clutching. "You'll be all right, just take the pills. We're all destroyed. We all have monsters and dead cats and hollow rooms, it doesn't run in families, it comes from being alive. You have to be strong, you have to have a sense of humor."

"Can I have a cigarette?" I scream at him. "Please, get me one, I'm scared, I'm terrified, she couldn't get the smoke. The train went much too fast for her, don't you understand, she was crying all the time talking to herself, but she was my sister, she was my sister. You can't know what I felt when I saw the cat hanging there, when I saw him standing next to it and I kept trying to clutch the sun bands to me losing them, standing there, losing the woods and childhood and not understanding. I didn't understand."

The Turtle gets out of bed, out of his sleep, and ambles across the room, fumbling in the dark for the pack of cigarettes. "You're hungry," he says, "you need to eat something, what do you want?"

"No," I answer him, "not hungry. I'm stiff and suffocating and weary, my whole body feels like a toothache. I don't want anything to eat, but thanks, don't leave, don't go away."

He lights a cigarette, I see the orange dot in the dark with him behind it looking out the window and thinking to himself, Not this again.

2

The priest is grinning at me, the great black shirt and face-
less full face are grinning at me. He's not real. Maybe he is
God, maybe he can save. The Turtle's brought him here like
a present, my turtle husband slipped away and brought me a
priest.

"Would you like to talk about it, my child?" he says, qui-
etly pulling down the window shade. "Would you like to sit
down next to me and talk about it?" taking me gently away
from the window and sitting me in the fat old army general
who is getting tired with all his cotton stuffing coming out.

"You see I need to love someone, father," I tell him while
he's watching me. "I tried to strike one up with Jesus but it
didn't really work, it was fragmentary, not essential, but I
really tried. I'm a freak, father." I begin again, "It's not
going to matter whatever you're going to say, because you
don't matter. There's a street down there that's asking me to
jump into her and end and it's up to me, you see, it's all up
to me, alone, all alone, again."

I'm fumbling in my pocket for a cigarette which makes me
feel more arrogant in front of him, makes me feel more out-
rageous and evil, makes me feel like he's a practical joke at a
time when I have no sense of humor left at all. He's another
big mistake, another rage because there's nothing in his pres-

ence for me but more obligations I can't meet, more silences I can't hear, more burdens I can't carry. He's more that's not real and I can't use more not real, more not real can't give me courage, only real can give me courage and now I have to carry him. The Turtle gave me just a little more of what can destroy me at the time it can destroy me best and fastest, just another gift to show his blindness.

Doing the waves on a surfboard, father, you can't imagine the sensation riding in on your mother's breast, a mother who never leaves you in the dark alone. Free-falling, rising to the top like a human bubble, copping hash from the junkie and selling it to the clergy, see the mother superior turning on father, what a gas, people who never smoked before, brand-new customers, and watching them, but they all say the same thing, father: "I don't feel anything." "What are you supposed to feel?" There's nothing to feel. "It isn't real. It's all a put-on, I don't feel anything." But they *never* feel anything, father, they have no feelings that's why, so how can they feel this, you need to know how to feel to begin with, wouldn't you say, father? Sometimes it's awfully real, wildly warmly real, arms around each other, purple pink and sloshing real. You get on and you fly over everything that binds you down and while you're on it's real, universally, oceanically real, you love to the nth degree of your soul all creatures who breathe and suffer and struggle, who are muddling forward backward just like you, just like me and us—all of us—you're one with all the aching in the universe and that is real. If you can't make it yourself, the drugs can make it for you, father, that's why I'm a drug dealer.

"She's not telling you the truth, father, she's lying to you, she's not a drug dealer, she's putting you on." (My turtle husband is betraying me to the priest.) My mother-husbandturtle is reproaching me gently in front of the Sunday school teacher for telling little fibs, wild little silly fibs, and to think, telling them to the sleeve of God, my turtle-motherhusband is trying to save me with all sorts of little poisons that come in all sorts of little pistols aimed at my brains, my mother-husband-turtle is an abomination to my soul. He keeps killing me and killing me with his nothing. But don't you see, I have to answer this way for his gift of a priest that he's given me. A gift like every other gift, an annihilation which I try to survive.

Honesty is as unessential as lies, I've told you the truth, father, the real kernel of my kind of truth is all in there. I've told you the truth although I haven't been honest, but honesty doesn't count any more than lies count, don't you see, it's all a matter of truth, and I'm giving you that and I'll give you more of that. I'm telling you that I'm a certain kind of freak. I live in a cave where there is a pool of ink-black water with water lilies blooming all the time, it's beautiful there, it's peace and dreamlike with a sand beach down to the water's edge where we can sit if you will come and visit me in better times, if there will be better times, and we can smoke a joint and you'll never have to think about it, about the thing between men and women, what it must be like. I can help you, father, I can show you what the thing is all about, you'll never have to think about it again, I can save you, father. You're a great black shirt that tells everybody just what kind of freak you are—a no-fuck freak—the one thing about you that is real is your nose. A great red veiny Irish drinking nose, a human nose that has failed, a nose of weakness that is human, the real part, the prideless veins that have succumbed to spirits, they needed something at one time, and in needing they have been weak and weakness is human so you have a human nose, bags under your eyes, big, full, fleshy bags, bags full of promise, who knows what treasures could be stashed away in those bags. I can't tell how much God you are or how much human, your nose and bags confuse me, but your great black shirt is there to shield you from all evil, lucky you, godlike shirt that you wear like a badge. What if I straddle you, father, and grab your hands and put them on my thighs so you can feel me pumping up and down, up and down? And you can watch, old Turtle, watch me make it with the priest, watch the father's face contort in pleasure, a real drug dealer fucking God, what if that's the only way to keep me from jumping, what if that's the price, can you do it for me? Saved by a fuck, while my husband-savior looks on in gratitude, my husband who later will give a contribution to the church in all his gratitude for exactly what I needed, the human thing, the profound touching, the cure of cures with the sanction of the church and God and man. How about it, father? Want a go at me? at flesh, at weakness, at needs that sometimes go unanswered in the night all wailing and hungry? Coming and coming and coming and coming into a woman not a handkerchief, no repentance, no remorse, just more and more and more, father, going down on me in my little nest of matted hair all wet from come juice, licking the insides of my thighs and tasting real woman, never tasted it before, going mad from the smell, the flavor, until you leap up and throw me down and pull my legs apart, plunge your uncircumcised member deep into me. I will start to menstruate for you, father, the blood of Jesus all over your half a cross, "Jesus, Jesus," you will scream as you fall all over me in one big heap of human man, past priest. I have this brother, father, he understands me.

My sister was beautiful, I was not. She was full grown, she had bosoms. Her hair was red, her face was light and clean and with the kind of bones that showed she came from good strong important people, people who all had good bones and strong chins, people who drank and people who failed— people who committed suicide. She wore wonderful clothes. She had a fur coat, she had pocketbooks and plaid slacks and perfume bottles with little silk atomizers from China or France, places far away. She was neat and she wore brassieres and garter belts and stockings. She had loafers and thick wool socks and closets full of evening gowns with satin appliqué and little spangles, with full tulle, fairy princess skirts. She had real jewelry. My father gave her real gold things

20

with stones in them and pearls and bracelets, an amethyst ring in a thick gold case around it for her finger. I envied her that ring. She looked like my father. She had the same build as he, the same color. They were all fair but me, I was dark and different and olive. They were all small and fair but I was big and dark like an Indian with these huge enormous eyes and greenish skin. I had no color, they were all a million shades of pinks and blonds and whites and red and rosy cheeks and freckles, not me, oh no, not me, I was always different.

I used to watch her, I thought she looked like a rose. She committed suicide, father, just like that, on the kitchen floor. What a family, you're thinking, what a nifty wholesome family, doing all sorts of interesting things, makes you stop and think a little, what went wrong.

The night is a black rider coming on a huge black horse bringing terror for me. Does it run in families? Where is it going to stop? With me this time? Does it skip a generation like TB? Who can save me, father, who can save me, who can save either one of us?

"For God so loved the world that he gave——" The priest is kneeling on the floor beside the television set.

"For God so loved the world that he made people and ruined everything, right, father?"

Ha ha ha.

Ha ha ha.

My sister never lent anything and she never borrowed anything either. She cried a lot, all the time she would cry, don't ask me why, don't ask me why I'm telling you about her either, I wasn't all that close to her, I liked her, she was my sister, that's all, but I hardly knew her, but you're here and I have to tell you something so you'll leave feeling you got something. I'm like that. My mother always told me how she hated to lend things, sweaters, shoes, pocketbooks. My mother said she had no humor, she was too sensitive, she cried a lot if they teased her, and they always teased her, my mother mostly. Still, in the nights when the house was quiet my sister would lie on my mother's lap and tell her all her secrets, all the things she did and who she did them with and she would make my mother laugh, that was her job, to make my mother laugh. She fell asleep with her head in my mother's lap, pleased that she had made my mother laugh, telling her all her secrets just to please. She'd do herself in to please my mother, but she never did, don't ask me why but she never did, my mother would still make fun of her and tease her and she kept crawling back and kept nestling into my mother's lap and kept on telling all her secrets anyhow. They found her on the kitchen floor one Christmas morning. How long ago? Don't know how long ago, she pumped twenty-five sleeping pills and half a bottle of bourbon into her, dead with the car keys in her hand in a nightgown and a fur coat, that's how they found her, with the amethyst ring on her finger, the one my father gave to her. I wanted that ring, I asked my mother for it the day of the funeral. My mother didn't want me to have it. "No," she shouted, "not you, not that ring, it's cursed, it's an omen, it's jinxed, not you, not you." That's what she said to me. "You're my precious one." I wasn't pretty like my sister and that's what made me precious. I felt ugly and green and skinny when my mother held me to close to her but I stole the ring anyhow and I have it, I kept it. Is it jinxed?

I quit school and moved in with the Turtle right then when things stopped mattering. A lot of things stopped mattering to me when my sister died. "Where did I go wrong?" my mother wrung her hands at me. "Dear God, tell me where did I go wrong, she's dead and you're a little tramp, a whore, a slut, sleeping with a man right out in the open, staying there all day and night, not going to your classes, disappearing for days on end with a man who you don't mean a thing to, what did I do to deserve this?" She clutched her pocket handkerchief at me, "Dear God, tell me, spare me, let me know. How could she do this to me, how can you do this to me?" Her face was red and swollen while she gave me this farewell speech, I didn't answer her. My heart was ripping in two but I didn't answer her, I just took the few things I could grab and ran away. I had to. Who knew where she went wrong? Who could find it and name it and wash it and hang it out to dry? It's just that it's so easy to go wrong.

It was marvelous to make love with someone new, someone brand-new who would watch me, every bit of me, it was wonderful. It made me come alive with him watching me, he wasn't my first lover but he was the best one, then, when it was all so new and sweet and happening like it did.

The great Turtle was always attracted to insanity, to illness and disaster. He thrived on it. It made him excited, all the sordid misfit strangeness, all the irregular meanderings of the body and soul, it was what he wanted. He wanted to clean it up and set it straight, he wanted to hear all the bedtime stories and he listened like a child to all the dreadful things about my mother and the silent house and what happened with my brother and it made him excited and it made him want to fuck and fuck, the more I told the more he wanted to fuck. That's how I purged myself and that's how he came alive, listening to these endless stories over and over again. And in the end he put his arms around me and told me he'd protect me, he said no one would ever hurt me again, no one could harm me, and I believed him. I loved him then. I thought I could keep him loving me while he was watching me—that I could care for him by telling him all of it forever, that this would be enough, that this was something we could build on, but it isn't. You can't build on disaster. The stories got stale. He wanted new stories, father, I had to find him new stories to keep him saving me and protecting me, to keep his arms around me in the night when I still wanted his arms around me in the night, but I don't anymore. I don't love him and I don't want his arms and this is death. I don't want him to gag me with his cock. He used to hold my head down there and gag me while he loomed over me, huge and straight and smiling with his eyes closed, and I would gag. He did this after he made me tell him again and again about the things that happened to me with other men. I thought it was strange but I loved the way he got all hot for me and wanted me, the way the stories made him come alive and he held me there and pushed it in so deep tears would come into my eyes and I would begin to feel so sorry for myself, so low and so debased and so crumpled, with his cock gagging me and I loved it, it cured me and put me straight and right and ready. When he loomed like that above me I was nothing. I was the lowest I could be and he could make me that or an infant baby at its mother's breast or a whirling black mist of feelings so intense that the bottom fell out of eternity.

It was winter when my sister died, the air was gray, the gray sky and buildings ached at four o'clock, not even tea and cookies could put the lights back on in the gray time when nothing grew and the world had gone to sleep and all the icy people hurried to get in. December. The cruelest month for the crippled and the crazy and the poor, for the torn and hopeless and the weary, the artists and the dreamers, it's the worst month, trailing warmth and green, moving into more warmth and green, an inverted death between two lives. That's when she died, father, and I've wondered so many times if I'd ever escape it, if I could grab the smoke she couldn't find.

"Why can't we get married, not really married but live together in a little house? I'll have a cat and a piano, you can do whatever you like, I'll keep house for you and cook and sew and do all sorts of nice things. People will never know we're brother and sister. Why can't we do like that in some far-off place—I've read about it, I've heard about such things, a spinster sister and a bachelor brother living together, why can't we?"

It was raining finally. A dark afternoon, the color of silver during the rains. The rains hadn't come for weeks, every-thing was brown and dry and cracking but finally they came in huge black clouds and dark, ominous skies. The rains came and flooded and poured and drenched the starved earth and made it live again, and made the desperate brush rejoice, made the young trees unafraid, made the dust melt into something possible again and we stretched across his bed and listened to it. The downpour began early that morning and until it came there had been a sorrow over the daytime. It didn't matter though, it was the sorrow of nature really, not a personal sorrow, not the sorrow inside myself, and that made the difference. The rains could purge me and cleanse me and purify me, they could make me weep just because it was finally raining.

"What if we got married and had a child?" I asked him.

He laughed. "The child would be an idiot, same blood makes idiots, that's what."

"But then you'll go away," I said to him. "You'll go away and leave me and I will be lost and nothing will be funny anymore, I wouldn't be able to endure it if you went away. You'll marry some flaky girl who giggles and wears her hair pulled back, some girl who's rich, like Mother wants you to, you won't love her, she won't make you laugh, but you'll marry her and have children and then what will happen to me?"

"You'll marry some jerk who works in a bank," he said, "some freak who wears his jackets buttoned all the way up, someone who shines his shoes and wears underwear, someone rich or worse than rich, someone whose mother's rich and has all the money and you'll have to go there for dinner on Friday nights and you'll have to take all the screaming brats with you and be polite. He'll probably have pimples and bad breath and bore you to death besides. He'll eat liverwurst and onions every day for lunch on rye bread and wipe his mouth twice when he's done with the paper napkin."

Then we'd start to laugh and wheeze and howl, a private language all our own, a secret understanding beyond intrusion from the outside world. We were on one side of the seesaw and all the rest of them were on the other. We made fun of the world, we poked holes into it, we watched the water gush out and we sloshed it up and spit it back in laughter. We understood each other completely. Ours was a union that had no strangeness in it, just the flowing into each other in a total sense of identification where there was no strangeness. There was never a time I didn't know him and know how to make him laugh, how to sidestep his darkness, where to find his quiet, how to quiet him and smooth away the roughness, how to ease him and taunt him into rage and fury, where to stop and how to twist him into bringing me a small bouquet of wild lilies clutched in his growing hand, into lining little ribbons for my hair on the bed, make him stop and stare at me and watch me move, the little gifts he left at my bedroom door without a word, his head hung down, some money in an envelope he'd give to me and disappear. He'd hold my head when I was sick and then got sick himself, and sit with me when it was thundering and tell me how it wasn't bad, whatever it was, he'd always say he'd make it go away and nothing could ever harm me as long as he would live. I loved him.

There was never a time we weren't crawling to each other on the floor, touching and looking and finding, exploring, discovering each other. We were twins lying in the womb together, from the very start we were cells together, seedlings together, crawling on the floor to each other again and again, smelling in each other that familiar smell, the depths of eyes that met again and touched faces, our fingers in each other's mouths from the very beginning. We had to be twins, lying on our backs and holding each other's fingers, hearing each other's thoughts, we had the same heartbeat, pulse beat, breathing. We were one person, we must have been, but we weren't twins, he told me; he was older, he was the boss of me, he always told me this and I believed him, I believed whatever he said.

Teasing each other into it, luring each other into it with little games and playing tag and touching from the first moments on rainy days when there was no one else around, all hidden away by the springhouse walls out there behind the house.

"Where are you?" she would call across the summer afternoons.

"Out here," he would holler back.

"It's time to come in and get washed for dinner," she would say.

"We're coming," he would say and I held my breath and he held his hand over my mouth so I wouldn't make a sound with him on top of me, pressing my body with his own, in full command, not afraid, with his hand over my mouth. How old were we? Ten, nine, eleven, thirteen, out behind the springhouse, in his room, on his bed, all the time, any time, every time until he went away. When did he go away? How can I never remember this? But one day he went away. He wasn't there. I looked for him and I waited but he didn't come that day or the next day, or the day after that, he didn't come.

"Where is he?" I asked her, but I don't remember what she said. He's gone, that's all I knew, he's gone.

Gone with all the dirty dancing into the center of the earth, the frenzied dirty dancing that he took with him, the smells that take you deeper and deeper, bleary-eyed and tired and hazy into all of it, into the big sucking up and swirling out that was ours, the vortex of the universe, a draining all in color, living under a waterfall of electricity, swirling, twirling, whirling, into that part of my body that was my voice and came to be my life long before it should, before it

27

was tinged with shadows and walls, before it was defaced by time and labels, before it was something open. We thought it was only ours, that we had invented all of it, that we were blessed freaks in possession of an enormous secret no one else had ever stumbled on, or ever would, when you first discover the secret of your body and what it's capable of delivering.

Down in the basement where there was a stained glass window that didn't look out, he would ask me if I heard him. Can you hear me? he would say, and I could hear him. The little windows with the lights coming through, the chipping paint and the wooden staircase, the broken banister in the almost dark. Can you hear me, can you hear me? Yes, I can hear you, I can hear you, I can tell you everything in the dark, and I never told him anything, I never spoke a word. It was mute and silent hearing, hearing each other in silence that was mute, a million echoes, and I could gasp for breath and keep on hearing him and feel it echo in my mouth and I could crawl into his darkest shadows and feel the sun. Then one day he went away. He was gone.

The cellar door was closed. The bedroom door was closed. The bed was made and never slept in anymore. The spring-house was dead, cobwebs caught my tears and gray sunlight made the dust that had no prints or unevenness, not anymore. Who would hold my head when I was sick, who would stand with me and hold my head? He was gone. Who would leave the little gifts at my bedroom door, little things with paper and a bow, give me money in a wordless envelope and read to me out loud at night? All of this was him. Who would I tell my secrets to and who would tell me not to cry? He was my mother and my father, my brother and my friend, he was my laughter and my lover, all of this was him. He was my secret and my self, something total from the very start without a stop or break, and he was a man and I was a woman when we were children, little children, and we were ageless and timeless and ancient and eternal.

Boarding school, holidays, summers, "He'd be back." Violin lessons, piano lessons, dancing lessons, school and dresses and dinners and no one there.

Fourteenth birthday, the house was filled with flowers, yellow flowers, the windows were open and it was spring. Your brother's coming home today. Spring vacation and your birthday—and there he was.

How long? Months. How many, many months long and without memories and he was standing there. His face had a bandage, he had been hurt, but he was standing there and something almost worse than all that had gone before was happening. He was afraid to look at me. This painful kind of embarrassment that was to happen so many times in the years to come. This mute something cringing, head hung low and hideous. And stories about school and stories about the boys and card games and making it all funny and about his studies and the airplane trip and what about college and maybe becoming a doctor or a priest, and the gambling and a lost suitcase and never mind, it's good to see you, wonderful, glad you're home. My grandmother was coming with a gold bracelet for my birthday, my grandmother was coming. My sister was flying at him, arms open, screeching and talking, so many words, so many smiling loud faces coming at him. My grandmother would be here soon, happy birthday, then he turned and looked at me. He saw me standing there and looked at me. It was quiet, like standing on ice that was about to break.

"Come upstairs with me, I have something for you." And I followed him without a word.

He was in control again the way he always was when she would say, "Where are you, time to come in for dinner," and he would holler back to her while he was on top of me with one hand over my mouth and I would hold my breath and he was in control of all of it again.

His room where I hadn't been for so long, where I dared not enter after I found he was really gone. I looked at him.

He was seventeen years old. He had a bandage on his face. We weren't twins, we weren't even friends, not anymore, everything that happened in the past was wrong, was done, was silent, without trace of its existence. We were proper brother and sister now with something to hide, something to never breathe a word about or allow to live for a moment ever again. It was done, more than done, it was to be denied by both of us to each other forever. This thing.

"You're all grown up," he said to me. "Fourteen years old today."

"Yes," I said.

"You look great, you're going to be a real knockout." I smiled at him.

"What have you brought for me?" I asked. "Is it something to wear?"

"It's a locket," he said. "I bought it for a girl at school, but I didn't like her all that much so I thought I'd give it to you."

For half a minute my heart stopped beating. My breath got caught in my chest. My face flushed, fury raged through me like a devastation. There were no words except—"For a girl at school, for a girl at school—" I looked at him and felt the sum of all my insides shriveling up and knotting. Hatred-kill. He looked at me and laughed, tossed the little box at me from where he was standing. The boy who tied me up and beat me with the branches of the trees, the boy who held my head when I was sick, swarming dizziness, swarming warm whirling in my head. I ran from the room, away away.

Running down the hall, down the steps, running through the foyer with the sunlight flooding it and making it all white and light, out the door into the garden with the sunshine and the low stone walls with the violets growing between the cracks, down to the springhouse and out beside the stream. I fell over on the grass, stretched myself full length across the grass and cried into my arms. There were no thoughts but floods and floods of tears, endless dams had broken, the silence of the last few months was shattered with the desperate sobbing, all that was bottled up and kept tight came flooding out into the air and I was strewn across the flow and carried by it.

The swan drifted by and he was standing next to me, the bandages were on his face. I looked at him. He crouched down next to me on the grass, put his hand on my head and stroked it. "Sh-h-h-h, sh-h-h-h, don't cry, not to cry, you mustn't cry like this," his face was knotted up in pain. "I was only kidding. I bought it for you, there was no girl at school, there was never a girl, it was always you, it was always you."

How many times, so many times, how many times, a million times in a million years, day in and day out, five years, six years, seven years, for always, and I was seeing him again.

"Grandmother's coming," he said, "she'll be here any minute." Urgency, the same insistent urgency was creeping into him. He rolled me over on the grass out there behind the springhouse and with his eye to the house, he undid his pants without a word, like a criminal with all his wits about him right before the meditated crime. He sprung on top of me, still with his eyes riveted on the house, and pressed me flat on the earth beneath me. I felt the urgency, I saw the urgency—he pinned me there and began to rock, his head was back, his eyes were closed, something trance-like blind was coming out his mouth, "You'll never get away from me, I own you, you're my slave and I'm your master, right? Isn't it right, you'll never get away from me, you're mine, you're mine, do you understand? You're mine." And he rocked and he rocked and he rocked.

No, it's not right, it's not right. I wrestled with him. I squirmed and tugged and pulled. A feeling of boredom, a feeling I would go mad from the boredom, although it wasn't boring, nothing boring, but boredom was destroying me. My grandmother was coming. I wanted her, I had to get away from all this boredom, where was my grandmother?

"Let me go," I squirmed and tugged and pulled and struggled loose and ran from him, all the way up the hill, all the way across the lawn, across the wooden porch, the screen door, threw it open and heard it slam me in.

And there she was, standing still and smiling safety at me, light was coming from her pores, a golden halo of stillness around her great black dress, standing there smiling silently at me. There were no words, just her face imprinted in my mind, her smiling silent face through all these years.

"Where is he?" my mother said.

"He's coming," I told her, "he'll be here," and I watched the things she didn't say, I watched her watching me, and her face had a strange and private little smile.

3

"We are without question," my mother said, "superior people." Her hands folded near her face, her yellow eyes large and stagnant, smiling, a drifty vague expression on her face, far away, unreal and dreamy. Her fey, eerie little things she had going with the other world. Her absolute illusion, her game. There was something glassy about my mother, something transparent and storybook. She was the fairy godmother that came and left with wings. She wouldn't break if you threw a rock at her. Her expression wouldn't even change. The rock in some magical way would bounce off and never enter the little sparkly world of dancing swans and fantasies where she lived herself away.

"Pass the butter to your grandmother, darling," she said to me, not looking. "Sometimes I even think we're a dethroned royalty living on old crushed velvet and tapestry. We're apart from the rest of the world, the rest of the world doesn't enter us, we are better. No one has our certain kind of wit and intelligence. Fourth generation, we're allowed to become a little decadent, decadence is really rather interesting, isn't it? My grandfather was an elegant gentleman when all those upstarts were just getting off the boat. I tell the children all the time they don't need anyone but each other, be close, children, don't trust strangers, trust each other, blood is thicker than water, believe me I know. It's so important to make them understand they have only got each other, no one else will ever understand them, no one else will ever really care as much." And she'd end the monologue and gaze adoringly at her own reflection in the million mirrors that lined the dining room walls. The entire dining room was made of mirrors with white wood and white floors, white table, white chairs with white leather seats. Great crystal candle holders held white candles with a crystal bowl in the center filled with crystal fruit.

In front of the mirrors were little shelves of glass with grille doors that housed little glass birds in glass cages with the mirrors behind them, little glass clowns and glass swans all in glass cases with mirrored walls reflecting and double-catching all of it until the room became some kind of visual echo around and around the table, catching parts of people and reflecting them again and again in the mirrors, reflecting finally themselves until there was double and triple of everything and everyone in parts and pieces like prisms or facets of a finely cut diamond, until you didn't see anything but the light and dark and a thousand little angles and nothing real. All this went all around the table, mirrors reflecting mirrors, around my mother sitting there in a yellow satin dressing gown with tiny seed pearls on it, worn at the elbows, stringy at the collar, threadbare at the cuffs with her long arms and lovely hands holding her face while she smiled into the mirrors reflecting parts of herself round and round the white and illusionary room. A torn ivory lace tablecloth with raggedy holes in it covered the table with the table peeking through saying none of it was so, it was all a lie, the table knew. The table was the only thing that was reliable.

Anna hobbled out of the kitchen carrying a silver tray with the copper coming up along the side. She had played the game a long time now herself. She usually whispered, she usually never said a word unless you asked her something simple and she would answer simply, but every now and then

Anna would go into rages and shout and scream and begin to weep and my mother would glare at her, the old black woman, and without another word Anna would be fine again, just as abruptly as she became enraged.

My brother would sit next to me again for this last time, silent. He would eat and leave the room and leave the house. I could see him through the dining room doors that looked out over the grass down to the stream that ran beside the springhouse, see him walking down and back, returning to the dining room and sitting down again. He came and went in silence. He listened to my mother's monologues but he wasn't sure, he was never sure, he never found out if she was right or wrong. Her voice never changed, her expression never changed, her monologues went on and on like the reflections in the mirrors all around her, like echoes on the wall.

A summer that was silently shattered and we all kept sitting there listening to my mother. A yellow-white aloneness hung around the glass birds and the dancing swans in crystal cages behind the gilt lattice doors, there was no conversation except my mother talking to herself about how no one was good enough for us except each other, her poison, her inbred murder, her disaster, while she grinned and posed and wet her lips and saw herself reflected, poor soul, poor little mother, poor wreck in a yellow satin dressing gown with threadbare cuffs and elbows, with yellow eyes that didn't see, that could only stop where the noise was coming from. Had she ever seen? What happened to her once that was so terrible it forced her into a world that wasn't real?

Inside myself there was still this restless sense of boredom, this pulling tearing wailing restless boredom that was squeezing me and gripping me with no way to escape. I looked at my grandmother. She was the post that I could grip that saved me from the undertow, my steadfast grandmother eating and chewing and putting butter on her little roll, dedicated to her meal. And I watched her and she stood out all in black in a white glass world that kept reflecting itself in a million little prisms all around the room. Only she stood out in black and real and fat and living around a piece of roll that she was munching.

Summer, an uncharted course of too much time and velvet days all done in yellow, white, and green beside the creek with the swan who didn't care, who drifted silently along, leaving no traces, needing nothing, indifferent. There were no secrets, there were no memories, a door was slammed closed on all the yesterdays, all of it was put into a box with hinges and closed and locked and gone. Having to start again with a new beginning. He was gone, he never came back after that summer. We were separate people moving separately in our own little space. My sister was married that summer and only I was left with daydreams that were so vague they danced by on chiffon wings which I couldn't net or hear, only drifting feelings that occupied my mind and made me stare into space and squirm but weren't clear or reachable.

School in the autumn was a window on the courtyard, school was a bird flying to the windowsill for a moment and then away. School was a part of the day where I jumped when called on for an answer. I never had the answer, I never heard the question. I carried the books and never saw the people sitting all around me while I was staring out the window. And then there was summer again when the heat was insufferable, nights when I couldn't sleep because the heat was so intense, being alone with myself and trying to find it all again with myself but it wasn't the same, it couldn't be the same and there were no memories that went with it, just the vague daydreams I couldn't reach, I couldn't form all done in watercolor washes that had no lines or end, drifting clouds over my mind in pinks and blues and yellows, smoke across my eyes that had no words to identify it all, no key for me or direction but staring mutely into more hot summer nights.

There were stick-figure boys who were becoming real who walked with me, boys who took me to parties and came on Sundays. Slowly boys started coming on Sundays and Saturdays and Mondays and Thursday nights and I watched them and I waited for them and I looked for them and I went with them. Slowly the fog began to lift, slowly the window shades of my mind flew up on a new day of boys who were laughing and riding motorcycles, drinking beer on picnics with their arms around my shoulder and something in me tearing toward them in a death-grip drive. I waited for them, for a certain one with long blond hair, or a certain one who walked a certain way. I waited for them in their cars and they kissed me. I got thin and long, my hair was to my waist, my face was small and waiting, I was silent, smoking cigarettes and waiting, one love after another, never lasting long, running to love and taking it all the way home for all I was worth with a closet full of dresses and slacks and wool socks and loafer shoes, like my sister had, and waiting.

The only friend I ever had was the girl my brother married. The girl we talked about on his bed, long ago, with her hair pulled back. The one who would giggle and be stupid. The one who had a lot of money. The train station was dark and empty, a kind of gray that railroad stations always are. I stood there watching from the steps, alone, so utterly alone, so raging inside all alone because he belonged to me, he did this thing to me, he dared to do this thing to me, to marry her. I stood there watching from the steps, everyone was waving and screaming and throwing rice at the train and they were in there waving back and smiling. I stood away, watching from the steps. They didn't see that I was there, he didn't notice. He loved her. He kept looking at her and it was clear he loved her. I cried that night like I did out beside the springhouse, only he didn't come to me that night, and I didn't stop crying that night, not even in my sleep. The feeling was an anguish so intense and so black, as though I was crying into a cave that echoed back to me and had no end, there was no end to the blackness. There was no end.

"Why won't you marry me one day?" I asked him. "What if we did get married or only live together, I'd have a cat and a piano, and you could do what you wanted to do, I'd keep house for you. I've read about such things, I've heard about such things, why not, why won't you say we can?"

"Our children would be idiots, that's what. Don't talk like that, things are bad enough the way they are. You'll marry some jerk who works in a bank and wears his jackets buttoned all the way up, some creep who wears underwear and his mother will have lots and lots of money and you'll have to be nice to her. He'll have millions of pimples on his face and it will serve you right."

"You'll marry some silly girl who wears her hair all pulled back and who giggles and you won't be able to stand the giggling, someone stupid—you'll see."

And we laughed and laughed and laughed, our own special understanding. On his bed that day when the rains finally came and soaked the world and drenched the earth, the teeming thundering swelling rainstorm day that might have made me weep. But now I cried into a cave that had no light or end, there was no end to my devastation when he married her.

4

My sister's funeral was as unreal as my sister's death. It was very peculiar that my sister was dead, peculiar and inconvenient, a disruption in the flow of living, a thing that brought my mother's tears and wailing, a thing that made me stand there wondering if I could have saved her, if I had only known her, if I could have done one thing, taken her with me—said something that was tinged with enough courage to have pulled her through that set of moments till it passed, walked the night with her and told her it happens like this to everyone but it passes. It can pass. That all you need is a little time to catch the train, if you can. But she couldn't even catch the smoke.

It was raining. Everybody was dressed in black out beside the grave. My sister's husband was screaming not to bury her. Not to take her away from him. My brother jumped on him, grabbed his throat in a kind of wild, unreal passion and started choking him and yelling how he killed her, how his lies and neglect and deceit were the causes of her death until my father reached over and pulled him away. In his stoic never-really-there way he silenced my brother's madness without a word. It was all happening like a dream, like a movie that I had paid to enter and watch except for a fleeting feeling that came to me of realization that my brother had known my sister and had cared about her and that I had not. They had some kind of relationship, some kind of bond which I was totally unaware of. It occurred to me then that my brother had known a lot of people, had friends and feelings and a lot of worlds going on around him, and I had not. All I had were the daydreams I couldn't reach or name.

He was an architect living in a city in an apartment and it was real. He was real somewhere, doing things that touched people, buying food and shaving in the morning. Going somewhere and telling someone something and hearing other things that people said to him. All of it was real. He had a wife. He was anchored. He was part of a world going on around me that I couldn't touch. He lived in touch with people, now with my sister's husband, once with her, in concern and in command, and he could make things happen and he could be affected and this amazed me. This was the only meaning my sister's funeral had. Why didn't I feel something, but I didn't. I didn't know her. Her life was as meaningless as her death. She never liked to lend things, that's what my mother told me, she never liked to lend things to anybody. I went and spoke to the swan about it after she died. I told the swan how little she mattered to me, how sorry I was that I felt nothing, not even sorrow for her. The swan was getting older. She stopped and listened to me now, she came for the crusts of bread I brought and stayed with me by the water's edge and listened. The swan seemed sorry that my sister died. She wasn't quite so indifferent and she stayed near me in her drifty peace and listened.

"Does it run in families?" I asked my brother afterwards. "Do you think it runs in families, heredity or something?"

"Don't be an idiot," he said, "it doesn't run in families. It's a thing, that's all, just a thing that happens. A bad, terrible thing."

"Why did she do it?" I asked him afterwards.

"She did it because she wanted to die," he said. "She

didn't want to live anymore. She had that right, didn't she?"

I didn't say anything more to him because he was angry. He was furious and dark. He always was when something wasn't good, when something wasn't funny. He didn't like it and he got nasty and biting and quiet.

"Who will take care of you, old swan, when I'm gone?" he asked the creature circling in the water. "Who will remind you of your happy youth when everything was green and you didn't have to bow your head?"

He took the bourbon bottle from his jacket and offered her a sip and started drinking. "Tell me, swanny, where will you go when they sell the house and new, strange, ugly people come to live here? Where will you go? Who will feed you popcorn and bread crusts? Not I. I'm going away, but I'll send you postcards, swanny girl. I'll tell you all about it when I have the time to write. This house is death and I have no romance with death."

What did he look like then? He was thin, his face was craggy, his blond hair fell straight across his head still, always in his eyes. He wore the same tweed jackets and narrow pants and the same blue cotton shirts with his tie open at the neck. His hands were beautiful. You might see him on a morning train or in a bar or walking down a city street in fall and you wouldn't notice him except for the war. There was a war all across his face and in the way he stood, some war he waged all the time, some arrogant war, his war, he woke up with it in the morning and drank with it all afternoon, and at night he went to bed with it still raging under his lips, under his eyelids, his war with everything around him all the time.

But he had marvelous plans in those days. Great cities made of little cardboard blocks, different colored roads and parks and cities all on drawing tables stretched across great light-filled rooms, and everywhere there were plans and papers and pencils and blueprints and ideas. He was good, he had to be the best, the most marvelous. Someday he would make the whole world just the way he wanted it, he could do anything, write stories, paint pictures, even change the world.

Did you notice, swan, the way he moves around still in command of everything? You should have seen the way he walked with my mother, the way he held her arm and whispered in her ear. And she clung to him, that's what my sister's funeral meant to me, the way my mother clung to him. I watched his wife, the way he was with her. It isn't going very well with them, you can tell, she makes him mad, the things she says, he walks away and you can tell he's mad. But he's working, swan, he's designing and building and being paid for it and that's something wonderful. He can take care of himself. I noticed that, that he can really take good care of himself. The world isn't foreign to him even with his war that leaps out of him, but he gets on top of it again. He isn't lost like I am. He didn't turn out to be a hobo or a bum, a seedy drunk, nothing like that. You would have been surprised how well he knows all about the world and how to live in it. That's what her funeral meant to me and that I didn't know her and that he did.

I'm still drifting with my head just above water trying to find something all my own that comes from only me. Everything else is an oppression, everything else is meaningless. I'm still dirty closets and furious bureau drawers, cobwebs and chaos, and the dream that has no end or harmony. I'm still hanging on his coat sleeve and floating out to sea searching all the time for something all my own, and always drifting back to where he is. No matter where he is, I'm always going back there, lady swan. I'm not at all like him. I haven't even begun to find my way. And do you know, he really has found his.

After my sister's death, I almost forgot what she looked like. All the pictures of her were gone, all her clothes and things were gone, nothing was left anywhere to remind my mother of her. She left no children, no letters or important things she collected that might have shown who she was. She took everything with her, but my brother knew her and said she was good. My mother said she never loaned things and when she died, all of her was gone. Maybe I could have walked it off with her, I often think, maybe if I were with her I could have put my coat on and made her walk till it passed, but I didn't know her, I didn't know she was even suffering. Does it run in families?

The priest turns away from me and looks at my turtle husband standing there and listening to all of it as he's heard it all so many times before. The Turtle smiles at me.

"You'll be all right, everything's going to be all right."

But what does all right mean? What is this thing all right? I don't understand.

I see the world as an empty place alone and that I've been cut in half, always searching, always looking for something and never finding it. I've come close a lot of times but then it's nothing again, it always turns into nothing but the search. I mourn for something I can't name, I hunger after something phantomlike, something always just around the corner that's never there. I get dressed up for it, I comb my hair for it, I brush my teeth and take my vitamins for it but it's never there. I never thought I'd live this long anyhow, I always think there isn't time, I used to think I'd be dead by the time I was twenty-one, that coming home one icy New Year's Eve on some slippery highway the Turtle, who never makes mistakes, would by some strange, unaccountable accident go into a tree, drunk, angry, who knows why, but I'd be dead. It never happened and I'm still here. For what reason? No reason, I can't find a reason except to chop off all my hair as soon as it gets long and wonderful. I chop it with a pair of toenail scissors and look at it on the bathroom floor, that's where it belongs, I think, what's the difference.

There's nothing wrong with the Turtle, he's good, he's

kind and decent. He bothers with me, why does he bother with me, why does he ask me not to cut my hair?

When my sister died I moved in with him. I think I told you that. I was at college then, my brother was sending me money and I could have stayed. They even offered me a scholarship but I couldn't be alone, I couldn't be by myself enough to stay there. I couldn't concentrate after my sister died. I wanted a child. I wanted to have a baby tugging at my breast. I wanted to give birth to the new savior in a manger in Times Square, televised with station breaks sponsored by your local Chrysler dealer, it didn't matter.

The priest shoots a look at the Turtle standing there and the Turtle shrugs his shoulder and looks at me, "Not this again."

You see, I continue telling them, someday the swan will die and then there won't be anything, absolutely nothing will be left, and so I've brought her here to stay with me. It's marvelous how she's managed to adjust to city living, living in small quarters. Every morning I fill the bathtub for her and she stays there for an hour or so, then she eats the crusts of bread and sleeps, she sleeps a lot these days, naps and little dozings, it's a shame, but of course she's getting old.

I have a fine veterinarian who comes weekly to check on her. He says I've done marvelously by her. I tried to tell him I had to, she is my hold on all things real, she's all I have. I don't think he understood this, I think he was just impressed with the job I did. You know, keeping a swan alive in a city apartment.

I would like to have a child with you, father. By some unusual means I would like right now, today, to have a wonderful conception with you. I should like to give birth to a great new shiny messiah, a wondrous son of almost God, who knows, maybe even God, a boy child, father. Would you like that? I don't want to offend or upset you, holy father, so that if you would like to put your globby stuff in a little prayer and send it into me maybe we can try it that way, any way, any way you like, who knows, I believe in everything. I have no doubts about anything really, any way you like I'm willing to try and then the brand-new messiah can come along, a manger in Times Square, televised with station breaks, wouldn't it be marvelous, father, and we shall have the child and he shall save the world and maybe even me.

"Everything will be all right," the Turtle says, and I look at him without a way to answer. There is nothing else to say.

"He's a turtle," my brother said to me. "He's a thick oxtail turtle. You can do better. There are a million better ones than him. Why did you pick this slow-footed, slow-walking, slow-thinking turtle? Tell me that. He doesn't do anything. He isn't, that's all, he just isn't. You think because he's really huge and hard-shelled, he's something, but he isn't."

My brother turns his back to me to light a cigarette, cups his hands to keep the wind out, and keeps on walking. He walks fast and I watch his face change expressions when the wind hits him in the eyes, watch him fight the wind and walk right into it.

"I love him."

"Do you?"

"He's good to me. He's huge. He's so big and huge and when it's windy I can hide behind him and not have to feel the bite."

"That's enough reason to marry anybody, anyone at all, but you're going to feel the bite, you're an idiot. Do what you want, it's your life."

"I'm safe with him. I want to be safe, you see, I really want to be safe inside. I want to feel my limits and my space. I don't want too much. I don't want to get all lost and not know where I'm going, or what I'm doing. I want a tight schedule. I want a lot of things tight and iron-metal straight."

"It's your life," he says. "Marry him, it won't make any

difference. You'll be married twenty times. How many men have you lived with already? How many men have you slept with—can you still count them on two hands?"

Silence.

"When did you start? When you were fifteen, when you were fourteen? When did it begin? Who cares when it began with you? I don't. I don't give a shit, it's your life, but if you ask me, I'll tell you, you're all fucked up. It doesn't matter who the hell you marry, why do you bother asking me?"

We were walking. It was night. He was angry. His marriage was over, he walked out on the flaky giggle with her yellow hair pulled back. Smoking a lot of cigarettes, drinking a lot. He fought with people at red lights and stop signs, he got into fist fights in bars for no real reason. He lied more than he told the truth, not outright lies, but stories, these fantastic sagas of who he was running with these days, the women who were chasing him and what he did with them and how it was happening, but they were all lies. I knew it. He told them to me. Most of all he was telling them to me, and I listened, not sure if he knew at all that he was lying. I wondered if he knew the truth himself, if they were really lies or delusions; to me it made no difference what he said, I understood him, I understood his lies, his wars, and his defeats.

There was a building that he had submitted drawings for and if his plans were taken he would have the chance to finally begin to change the world, his own building, his own monument. "Eight fountains all around it," he said, "and every day I'll go and sit there and just look at it. All mine." He had such enormous dreams and drive and needs. That's where he was. That point when he came back again for just a little while, his marriage done.

"Hey, swanny girl," he said, "you didn't get a card from me but just you wait, just you wait, old swanny girl, it won't be long."

He was still clogged on his war, on all his unresolves that were smeared across him. But he was peeping out at life now instead of spitting at it. The possibility of his building was humbling him.

We walked that afternoon across the fields that came down to the stream and sat there picking grass, fumbling with little bits of leaves and mud in our hands and saying little things, all weak sentences, all apart, looking for a place. Our sister was dead, we understood, there was nothing more to say, his marriage done, and I was going to marry the Turtle.

"Let's go away," he said, "France, Spain, Ireland, just this once, once more. We'll have a ball, we can take our camera and you can paint and I'll write over there, maybe if I'm away I'll write a play. I know a bunch of wild people, you know, really something people, you'd like them." And he looked at me, a long steady look that held its breath, I felt it hold its breath and I withdrew. That sense of boredom coming back on me, that restless itching pulling sense of boredom leaping out of the stream, out of the air and invading me and I looked away.

"Come with me," he said, "we always wanted to do Europe once together, forget about the Turtle till we're back."

Spring and summer were stretching out ahead of us with green smells and warm invitations to escape, always the open hand of new summers saying come away. Over there was the springhouse, just over there, four steps away.

"I need a rest," he said, "my eyes feel like two piss holes in the snow. I'm beat."

He got up from the grass. We started to walk back to the house. His arm was around my shoulder, his head hung low, his hand was on his cock.

"This thing," he says, "this building, it's not the most important building in the world, nothing earthshaking or imaginative, but it's where the money is. I really want to be very rich." His arm still around my shoulder. We're exactly the same height. Funny how exactly the same height we are. Was he short or was I tall or were we both exactly right or wrong in a funny foreign silent world moving all around us?

"Maybe the only thing I really care about is money," he begins. "Maybe that's really where it's at for me. I've tried people, they don't work. So if all there is for me is a lot of money, a lot of buildings, I better understand it. I'm not glad about it, I'm not broken either. It's just the way it is. But I need to get away, I really need to get on a plane and just take off, take off with my little sister."

I didn't answer him. I didn't say a word.

It was almost dark when we reached the house, the night had settled like a sigh. It always seemed as if no one was ever there, that the house was always empty until a voice came out of all of it to say, "Where are you? Are you there?" and we would say yes, and the voice was gone again to nothing. No faces.

In the drafty old Victorian dining room he stood with his back to me, facing out at the shifting shadows on the lawn. He looked like a half circle in the charcoal light of night across an unlit room. His arms were around himself cradling his stomach, his head was down, his knees were bent as if he were suddenly in enormous pain, rocking back and forth with it, holding the pain, rocking with it, comforting himself, hunched over, all around himself. The steely thing was gone again, the command, the mastery.

"What's the matter?"

"All in here," I heard. "All in here, bulging and sticking me in the guts, if I don't get away, if I don't get it out, I'll be destroyed. Something's eating me alive, what the fuck is eating me alive, it's been like this for, Christ, how long. I can't get my head together, I can't get my body to move and then it all comes over me and if I can't get it out, I'll be destroyed. Come with me, gotta get away, gotta get on a plane and go somewhere, don't marry that slob, for Christ's sake, for Christ's sake come with me."

I wanted to touch him, I wanted to put my hands on him, on his back that was toward me, waiting for me to put my hands on it. I wanted to make him better but I'd only make him better for a minute, what he had I couldn't cure, he didn't even want me really. He didn't know what he wanted but I couldn't help him. He was all alone, always all alone, the way I was, and being with me made his loneliness even more profound. Somewhere it had to stop for both of us, somewhere we both had to switch into other gears and drive in other directions. There was no possibility this way, no matter how it seemed or hurt, it wasn't possible, it was fantasy, all illusion.

Once we were two sides of the same thing split by some unreal mistake, but that was once and now I was going to marry the Turtle. But once we fused and merged and flowed into one another, nothing about the other was foreign, no words ever misunderstood, no feelings unforgivable, no moments remote, no storms unshared then, once, a long long time ago, and we both could see the springhouse in the moonlight from the long glass doors. I had to keep myself from looking there. I had to think of any other thing. I couldn't hear him. I couldn't let myself go loose.

"If they take my plans," he began, "if they buy them, and if we do the building and the fountains, maybe then we can go away, you and I, to France, yeah, France." He was standing up a little bit and looking blank ahead of him, his voice sounded like he was looking blank ahead of him, not seeing where his eyes were fastened on the springhouse.

"A house that overlooks the sea, and all the cats you want, you can paint the whole damn day away and all the dresses you can buy, anything you want. Don't marry the Turtle." His head falls back staring at the ceiling, his back to me.

"Hey, little sister, how would you like a house that overlooks the sea, how about that? I'll build it just for you." He spins around. "Of course they'll take my plans, they'll make the building and then another one and another one after that, I know they will, and then we'll get our house. Wait for me, baby. Wait until I do it all for you."

He grabs my breasts and pulls me up by them. He starts kissing me, my neck and face and hair, pulling me around the room by the nipples of my breasts, the gloom is gone, the lights are on again from deep inside, the night is over, swinging me around and around, singing and laughing and kissing me on the neck and nose and swinging me with him and I'm laughing with the tears coming streaming down my face, sobbing, laughing with him all around the room and laughing and laughing and laughing.

"But what if I don't?" A curtain drops, suddenly there is a brick wall flat against us, a dead end. He slouches in the windowseat and pulls the sweater neck up to his eyes and peers at me and not a word.

"What if, God forbid, they don't take my plans," he says from way down deep inside the sweater. "What if they take someone else's and it never happens. What if I fail, what then, little sister, tell me, God almighty, what will happen then?" Big pink tears are brimming over and falling down and being gobbled up by the sweater neck pulled up right beneath the eyes.

"They'll take them, you know they will, you know you always get what you want if you want it bad enough. That's what Mother always said, if you want something bad enough, you always get it. Don't you?"

His eyes brim silent tears all streaming down his cheeks. The sweater neck is catching them as they keep on coming in long thin lines now.

"And what about the Turtle?" comes up muffled from deep inside his orange sweater. "What about him?" His eyes are down, not looking at me, looking at his knees.

"I'm going to marry him," I tell my brother, not looking at his face, can't look at him, and he doesn't answer me.

It was a tiny wedding in the winter, a little room filled with white flowers, a desk and a judge, with the white snow falling against the window.

I married the Turtle in a dreamlike trance that wasn't real. Why was I marrying him, I wondered, for what reason? Who was the Turtle? Someone slow-footed and slow-thinking, someone who could hide me from the biting wind. It didn't matter. I was getting married because it was somehow time. I wanted the baby I was carrying. The Turtle's baby boy and I wanted to be away.

5

Ocean. Ocean. The ship is clipping over the ocean without a trace of effort or sound. The sea was black and deep, the moon was making light on the water, the stars made the sky sparkle like a thing of unset jewels on a velvet cloth. I was lost. I couldn't find myself at all.

The Turtle in new shoes. The Turtle reading a book in a deck chair. The Turtle sipping brandy and tipping waiters. The Turtle was never seasick, never had a bellyache, never felt a devastation that went by so fast it had no name but left you weak and clinging. But don't cling to the Turtle in his new shiny shoes. He walks too fast, too straight, too full of smiles. I'm lonely, why am I so lonely, forget it, look away, forget about it.

How many lovers have you had by now, my brother asked me then, that night—can you still count them on both hands? Were you fifteen or fourteen when it started with you, but I don't give a shit, it doesn't matter anyhow, you'll be married twenty times. He cupped his hand to light his cigarette and I watched the way he walked into the wind, the way his face would change when the wind hit him right between the eyes.

There weren't many lovers, I should have told him, just a few, one whose name I never knew one summer when the city was hot and the sidewalks were scorching to my bare feet. Who was he, in a dark town house tucked up behind the big imposing city mansions, who was he, dark hair and thin and easy? I stayed with him whose name I never knew, whose bed I never came out of, who I never saw again after two days in that little house. He was the first, a stranger. Who was he? Maybe he was you. Maybe he was always you, a million you's, all of them, but I shouldn't tell you that. Yes, you were right, fifteen that summer when it was hot, so hot, I couldn't help myself how hot it was. Don't be mad at me. I couldn't think it away. I couldn't get rid of it all by myself. I tried, God knows I tried. I was loyal to you, you must believe me when I tell you I was loyal to you, but it was so hot that summer that I couldn't help myself.

Did you love him? Would you ask me that?

When I was with him I loved him, yes, I really loved him when I was with him, but when I went away I didn't look for him again. I didn't want to find him anymore.

And was it good with him?

Was it good with him when you were fifteen years old in that town house? Yes, it was very good with him when I was fifteen years old in that little town house with the unmade bed and the sink full of dishes and the mess and window shades that never came up, the light bulbs without the shade, something almost slummy about it and it was very good with him.

And do you think about him still?

Yes I do, I still think about him and when I do, I love him. It was a smoky sort of summer heat with him, there weren't many words exchanged—just heat for heat in there and something hungry and nameless and dark. He's joined hands with you, he's standing next to you to form a human chain, a human link that leads out, out of the heat and loneliness into a warmth and a building block of what I've had that was good, it was a good summer, maybe I saw him again after that, I don't remember, maybe there were other two-days and

53

other nights. I don't remember but it was good and warm and real that summer when I was fifteen. Shall I tell you that, would you hate to hear it all, would you like to know the truth, it was good.

And then what? You can tell me, he says, I'm your brother.

Then there was another one, someone who was funny who I didn't love at all but he was funny like you were funny and we used to laugh like we used to laugh and he loved me. We went to places like the movies and to eat and drink milkshakes, we drove to the shore and walked on the beach and he loved me. He used to kiss my hands at red lights. It was nice. I liked him. He was religious. He went to church a lot and prayed and thought he might become a priest, only he was too funny for all that. He studied hard and had a parttime job, and he loved me. He bought me little books of poems and a garnet pin. I wanted to sleep with him but he didn't think it was fair to me, something like that, and so we didn't, it didn't matter all that much, not then, not at that time, it really didn't matter. We had other things and it was good enough. Until one night for some reason I had to sleep with him, I had to, that was all, and so we did, and it was all right, nothing great and splendid, nothing more or less than what I could do alone but because it mattered so much to him it became important to me, too. We were lovers for a year, I guess; it got better but it was really never all that great, it just got better, that was all. He loved me a lot, he put a lot into it, it used to make him cry and shake with love and want to talk about it all night long, but I was cheating on the side on him, only twice with a boy who worked in a gas station, terrible isn't it, the truth, the awful thing of truth, how I would love to tell it all to you, but I couldn't, could I, you could never bear to hear it all. Then I met the Turtle.

"Why are you going to marry him," you asked me, "why him, slow-footed and slow-thinking, there are millions out there better, why him?"

"I want the baby. I really want the baby. I've wanted the baby for a long long time and now the time is right and so I'll have it. Now do you understand? I need to have the baby."

"But why?"

"I can't answer that, but will you be with me when the baby comes?"

"Yes, I'll be with you when the baby comes."

"And will you love the baby?"

"I can't promise that."

"Where are you?" the Turtle asks me, grinning.

"I was away," I tell him, "but I'm back now. I was only thinking."

"Where are you when you seem so far away?" he asks.

"Only thinking," I tell him.

The Bay of Naples is a cove of lights that cups the water, jewels flickering warmth on a velvet night. I'm restless. Something in me tearing to get out and fly. Who to fly with? The Turtle? He doesn't hear it. He doesn't fly. Get all dressed up and splash on perfume, put oil all over my body and sit and wait for him to come, but he doesn't hear it, thinks it's funny, nice, cute, but he doesn't hear the méssage. Throw the dishes out the cabin portholes, watch the Turtle start to laugh, not funny laugh but nervous, very nervous. Throw more dishes out the porthole. Throw the Turtle's shoe out, the new one, not both, just one. Watch the Turtle start to laugh and cry at once. Watch the Turtle dash for his other shoe, too late, it's gone, watch the Turtle start to hiccup.

Holland, Sweden, Rome, hot and orange, dusty hot and dry. We dig into a little tiny room and start to feel the baby kick and move, time to head for home, another ship leaving France on Saturday.

He's watching me, thin and young and blond, younger

than myself. Blue eyes watching me. In the dining room at night he's watching me from over there, starts something real boiling again inside me. I'm dancing with him in the great rooms, gambling with him in the grand salon, sleeping with him from two till dawn and back in bed when the Turtle starts to stir on a brand-new day. I'm alive again. I love him. It's good with him. He's not afraid of anything. He's free. He gives me my first toke of hash, something hazy and sweet while he sings to me and I write a letter to my brother telling him how good it was, what it felt like, that it was something he should do. It's always like that, the first person I think of when the steak is good, when the wine is perfect, when I find something new and wonderful, to tell my brother.

"Where are you again?" the Turtle asks.

"Just thinking," I tell him.

"What are you thinking about?" the Turtle says.

"Nothing special, just thinking."

The pains begin first every five minutes. Something so all alone in childbirth, so white with a clock on the wall, the ticking echoes through my bones. "Hold my hand tighter," I ask him, "hold my hand," and he holds it, his blond hair falling in his face. His blue eyes avoiding me, he can't bear to look at me in pain. "Hold my hand tighter," I scream at him, "tighter, tighter. The pains are coming faster, don't leave me, please don't leave me."

"I won't leave you," he says, "I won't leave you."

"Make them help me," I beg him, "make them help me, please."

He goes and they help me into blackness and when I see again, my mother is standing there and the Turtle is standing next to her, a boy, a boy. I look around the room but he is gone.

"Where did he go?" I ask them. "Where's my brother?"

"He just left," my mother says, "but he'll be back, it was all a bit too much for him, but he'll be back."

"When's he coming back?" I ask her.

"He's coming back," she says.

We put the baby in a basket and went everywhere together that summer, my brother and I, while the Turtle was driving himself into a silent world that was all his own, that didn't matter to me very much at all. When he was there, my brother was away, when my brother was there, the Turtle found any other place to be.

A party in a great house high on a hill with steps in the gardens and hedges and statues, stone goddesses holding baskets of stone flowers. Fountains and marble walks where parrots were kept in cages tended meticulously, immaculate parrot cages for arrogant, high-colored, spoiled birds who viewed the outside world with disdain and squawked their high-pitched contempt hanging on a wrought-iron fence upside down.

"I have this brother," I told her, I told the girl who was giving the party. "Can I bring him along? He's in from Arizona and getting over an ended marriage, so can I bring him along? He's my architect brother who's going to change the world."

Who was she? Then she was nobody, fat and rich, so rich, so boring—but the parties were wonderful, we loved feeling so rich like we always felt when we were at her parties, swimming or playing tennis or eating out on perfect terraces with little poodle dogs running around with red velvet hair ribbons, waiters and butlers and maids who never said a word. It was great fun to be there, to see her skinny ugly mother leering in the background, watching with a fixed smile and all the young rich people, young aspiring social science majors creeping up to her and engaging her in simple little conversations to prove that the main reason all of them were there was to get in deeper in something very good, very rich, very full of very important contacts, it couldn't hurt and

these young social scientists were practicing a lifetime's train-
ing and now was their big chance, smiling, laughing, sucking in deeper and deeper till it was lunch and another
climber had his turn. The ugly mother stood there and expected it and relished it and preened for it. The daughter was
a girl I knew from school, she was fat and cried a lot. In recess
when we played jacks and I always beat her, she cried a lot. She
always cried when she lost and big things gobbed out of her
nose and her eyes spurted and she drooled. Her hair was
kinky blond and her cheeks looked as though someone had
stuffed them with cotton balls that she was too slow and too
defeated to have reached in and pulled out. She had no body.
Her shorts cut her thighs and left red marks. She wore over-
blouses to hide the bulges as best she could. She ran like an
elephant and her bosom was this huge enormous grandmother thing held up by steel.

"I'm going to marry her," he said.

"Why?"

"Because she's so rich and everybody wants to marry all
that money, so I will."

Then she got thin, after they got married she got thin and
she moved away with him, and he was good to her and she
blossomed while he was good to her.

He finally made the blueprints for his building and sold
them to a builder. I got letters and calls telling me how all of
it was beginning to happen for him and his calls came twice
a day and three times a day, and sometimes five times a day
or seven, and I waited and I held my breath waiting for it all
to happen for him, and it did.

"Don't marry the Turtle." That night in the dining room.
"Wait for me," he said, "a house that overlooks the sea and
all the dresses you can wear, a cat, as many cats as you want
and you can paint the whole damn day away."

And now she'd share it all with him. He'd buy lockets for
her and hold her head when she was sick, and he'd walk with

58

her with his arm around her shoulder and his hand on his cock. He needed a lot and she would give it to him and he would take it from her. He needed such an awful lot, and she, who ran like an elephant, with her navy shorts making red marks on her sausage thighs, her, with the gobby stuff running out her nose, she was his wife now and she would give it to him, she'd struggle for a lifetime to get to where we only began, she'd lie there on her back and make a little noise and feel a little twinge and think she was part of the great community of married and he'd roll over on his back and make himself come five more times before he fell asleep and she wouldn't understand and pretend she didn't notice and he wouldn't care if she saw or not, and they'd have a baby, and dinner parties and walks in the park when there was time, and he'd stick it in her mouth and her eyes would well up with tears and she would gag and he'd say, "Suck it, baby, suck it now," and she would pull away and run into the bathroom and retch and say she was sorry and he would laugh at her, he'd stand there and laugh his heart out at her and go out for a walk and his cock would always be hard and his hand would always be on it, when he said hello to someone or when he was walking in the park, when there was time, but it didn't make any difference, there'd never be a woman for him really, except me. So he'd work. That's really all there was for him now, work. But then I didn't know that was the way it would be. Then I thought there were endings to things, chapters and circles closed. I didn't know that nothing ever ends—only new beginnings but nothing ever ends except the search.

The little dog was dead. The Turtle carried him up the long driveway in the early evening. The child followed looking at the little black and lifeless body of the dog he loved so well. The neighbors' children gathered around the Turtle carrying the dog. The little girl turned and ran away. Two neighbor boys stood by the car crying without their hands to hide the tears on their faces, they simply stood there sobbing openly. The oldest neighbor boy helped the Turtle put the dog in the car and throw a blanket over him. The big dog who ran with the little dog through so many summers stood by watching. She was still and watching while the neighbor boy helped the Turtle put the little dog's body in the car and throw the blanket over him. The big dog stood there watching until the car pulled away, then she dropped her head and vomited into the grass. Her body was trembling.

We walked through the summer afternoon, a tan road over yellow fields that bloomed green and purple under a golden sky. The little boy walked next to me in silence, the big dog followed us, defeated. There was nothing to say. Just that the little dog was dead.

"Would you like to come into Mommy's studio today, just today, as a special treat?" I asked the little boy. His eyes lit up. "Yes," he said, "all right," eager, waiting to get in there where he was never allowed to come. This was my world, this was mine alone. No one ever came in here.

In here colors were blooming life, wet canvases, frames, clay, easels, life. In here falling from the ceiling, hanging from the glass walls, all over everything, life, in colors and shapes, all over everything, hanging, falling, stacked and strewn, life, disorder, chaos, all mine, all life, my life in this place where the world slipped away, where there was no trace of anything but me, my art and my fantasies. The smell was mine, the look was mine, the whole room, one long, straight, glass-lined room was mine any way I wanted it with a coffeepot and a bed and a radio, a place for a model to sit, a table with special things on it, things I liked, only the very best of things could come in here to stay, my place, my hiding spot where I could lick my wounds and recover from almost anything. This was the studio where it all happened for me, where I could get lost and not have to find myself, where the world slipped away and disappeared and time went into the cracks that held the glass together, my own private world of oblivion and escape.

"Let Mommy paint you today," I said to him and he climbed up on the wooden stool to sit for me. Often he wouldn't sit for long, but today he could. The golden hair all falling in his eyes, the fat apple cheeks, the fleshy hands, I could paint him blind, even if I had no eyes at all, I could paint him.

PART II

6

The ship sailing for Europe when I carried him inside me. No one knew then that I was pregnant, no one could have suspected it, the way I danced and swam, flinging myself and looking for everything all the time, and he was in me growing. The small German man who followed me and asked me for my underpants, to leave them under his pillow in his stateroom, would I leave them for him and I didn't, wrong of me, wrong of me, I should have left him the pants. I should have understood. Freaks, freaks, we're all freaks. The priest on the ship prayed for me. He did me a novena. The Turtle picked him up in the bar, of all the people on the ship the Turtle had to pick up a priest, my skin tingled in rage about it, I remember, my skin burning in fury. He looked at me like I was intruding on them, on the two of them, the Turtle and the priest.

"How do you do, I'm a dirty little filthy sinner. God have mercy on my dirty filthy little soul," and I extended my hand. But priests always make me feel like that, or worse, like nothing. The priest on the ship was drinking bourbon. The Turtle was sipping Scotch, they were discussing theology. "Hmmmmmm, yes, and do you think, hmmmmmm, no, and I don't think." I would sit there and watch them and think it was a restless agony—intolerable. That life was dangerous, absolutely, it was very dangerous. That's why they had armies and police and priests, all to protect the body and soul, great armies of soldiers and police and priests, stalking the world for danger, they could lick it, wipe it out, make everything all safe and sound and orderly, a nice and snug protected world if they had their way, a guarantee for the scared, spooked people who were good and law-abiding. But what about me? What about all the me's? Who would protect us? Not the police, not the soldiers, not the priests, no sir, never. We had no rules, we had no protectors, we had no one to show us the way, we have to find it all alone, groping and more scared, more spooked, more unsure of everything. Would it always be just this side of disaster? What is salvation? Where is the great black and white world the Turtle has, all safe and saved, talking to a priest? They both have a black and white, but me, it's always all gray and muted and diffused. I could understand it, good and bad, without judgment, without direction, it never mattered to me all that much, the way that other people did things, the things they did and how they did them, it wasn't my affair, and I couldn't imagine how they could care that much about my way, it wasn't theirs, all I ever had to tell me was my brother, that was my direction, that was my path, that was my protection. Him, all in him, where was he when things got so boring I writhed and stretched and fidgeted hours and days away, where was he, God, he would know, he would always know.

"We're really different," my mother used to say, "not like ordinary people, maybe better, really maybe better."

"But Mother, I have no rules, there are no rules, you never gave us rules, we need them—I'm in danger, Mother, do you hear, I don't hear the Turtle anymore."

"What are you thinking?" the Turtle asks, putting down his Scotch. "Where are you?" I'm still looking for him, restless, shall I tell you that, shall I tell you that in every face I'm looking for the falling yellow hair, in every bar, in every corner of every room, I am still looking for the boy, the boy.

Where is he? Discontented, moody, looking for him everywhere I am, but it's never him, old Turtle, it's always you and a priest, you and a pair of shiny new brown leather shoes just right, your jacket buttoned up. Why, why, why doesn't it feel like that with you, why did I ever have to know what it could be like then, when it was all in bloom, and green and cotton panties, him on a bed out in the grass? You've never known the way it can be, it really can be something unimaginable, and you've never known it, like most of them have never known it, and you're blessed.

I try to find it on every face, invest every new face with the possibility, every smile, think they are looking for it too, that way, the way it sometimes is, but it's only a memory, don't you understand, only a memory that's left on a night train going backwards into hell with the last stop apathy.

"Will you come to confession in my cabin in the morning, child?" the father asked me smiling.

"Go," the Turtle was nudging me, "it'll do you good."

7

Forgive me, father, for I have sinned. I confess I loved a boy when I was young and he was young and his face was full and his eyes were these enormous jet-black buttons. He used to come after school on his bike with all his books in the basket and he loved me. I confess I was the first girl he ever loved. I confess we used to fuck under the dining room table or on a stool in the kitchen when we knew people were roaming around the house late at night. That was half the fun, the scary part of almost maybe getting caught.

But I confess just when it was beginning to start with me, something inside shouted, "Stop, don't feel a thing, stop, don't feel his love for you, don't feel love for him when he feels love for you, only when he goes away. That's the only time that you can feel a thing for him at all, when he's not there." And I confess I would stop and I would let him fuck me and I would watch his face and see it all on him, the way it felt and the way he pulled me to him and stared at me but I didn't feel a thing. I wonder if he knew I never felt a thing.

Sometimes when we would be walking in the woods or down beside the stream I'd run away from him and he would chase me laughing and I'd stop and he'd reach out but then I dashed away. I'd take off my blouse and my breasts would be bare and he'd grab and I would laugh and he would chase me, reaching for my breasts, and I'd let my skirt fall down and all I would be wearing would be these little tiny under-pants and he would go insane reaching and grabbing and I would stand behind the trees and dash just to where he couldn't get me, where it was safe, and do you know, I never let him get me. Forgive me.

He would be so excited that it would hurt him and I still wouldn't let him get me. Then I would predict what would happen next. Maybe he would hit me with a switch that was lying on the ground—maybe he would take his belt off and whip me, but more, I thought maybe he might strangle me because he was so hot and so mad but still I wouldn't let him fuck me and he scared me when he was hot and mad like that and I laughed and I liked being scared and I kept on teasing him. I was always trying to see how far I could go, where the edge was in inches and specks. How to totter on the border and not to win and not to lose, just to totter. I wonder why.

I confess I used to play the violin when I was young. They thought I had a lot of talent, that I could really play the vio-lin. There used to be recitals with apple cider and cookies afterwards that they passed around and everyone was glad I didn't make mistakes or at least not big significant ones, just little mistakes that no one noticed.

I confess once I won a prize for playing the violin. Forgive me, father, but once I won a prize, a pen and pencil set when I was nine. I haven't really learned another thing since then, only that I've come to understand more and more the things I knew and that they were real, and they all had to do with people. I haven't really changed much since then either. Facts were boring to me, skills were pointless, and I stopped playing the violin because it didn't have to do with people. It was only repetitious boredom. It didn't fuck. I couldn't jam it up me.

There was this little man who came to my house on Thursday afternoons. His breath always smelled from on-ions. He was fat and gray and wore a moustache with white hair all around his bald head, and he would count, one and two and one and two, and he showed me where to put my fingers on the strings and how to hold the bow and where to put my chin just right and I would look at him and he would be intense about such little things and it all seemed as though it should be harder, more difficult, not as simple as it was. But it wasn't harder, it wasn't more difficult and it never got harder. Just little fingerwork and practicing with nothing shared, no secrets to be understood. Why couldn't things be really hard, really complicated where searching was necessary, where there were secret meanings to be understood, but there never were. In school the teacher would explain something and I would listen and I couldn't believe what she was telling us was as simple as it seemed. Surely it had to be harder, it had to mean more than what she was saying, I thought. Then when she asked us questions afterwards maybe she wanted more than feedback, maybe she wanted us to think and come up with something hidden, mysterious, remarkably tucked in there waiting to be released. But it was never like that. It was just feedback she wanted and it was all so dreadfully unimportant and easy and I had to wait for days till she went on to the next trick—there wasn't anything to it but the little tiny boring thing she taught.

I confess that while I waited I would imagine that in India the nine-year-old girls were married and having babies by now, that if I lived in India I could have a husband and a child and it wouldn't all be so boring and easy and dull, and I looked at the teacher from out of my windswept desert where Arabian men were bringing their horses to the watering holes, where the veiled women of northern Africa were walking to the marketplace peering out of chiffon wrappings at the men who stood against the ancient stone walls watching them and wondering about their private little mysteries tucked inside their dresses up at the top of their legs, and nothing was ever said. It was all exchanged in silence. I confess I didn't hear the teacher anymore or the little tiny things

she kept explaining for all that endless time that had no secret meanings or information having to do with fucking and
people. Everything but fucking and people, everything lifeless and still and boring was all she ever talked about and it
was like a gag in my mouth and a strap around my chest that
made me suffocate.

I confess I used to draw little pictures in the margins of
my papers. Little faces and bodies, naked men and women,
behinds and breasts and cocks with hands reaching for each
other, and when she'd come walking down the aisle where
my desk was, I'd cover them with my other hand and pretend
I was reading.

"Drawing obscene little pictures again . . ." and she'd
whip the paper from the notebook and smile at me, glad she
got her error for the day, her crime, her crumb of fallibility
to live on.

"Meet me after class in the detention hall," she said.

Detention hall—a long black room where there were
wooden benches and a table. Not a light could ever go on in
there where I would sit alone and wait for her to come preparing the worst torture ever known to man. Silences and
sneers and narrowed eyes with a black dress and the icy joy
of punishment.

"You're a filthy little girl," she screamed at me, "stand
up." And she shook me by the shoulders, rattling my body
till I was faint, or I was trembling in fear, and she never put
a hand on me.

"A filthy little girl who draws filthy little pictures while I
have my back turned writing on the board and when I turn
around you still don't stop, you keep on drawing those filthy
little pictures of men and women doing filthy little things together. I'm going to show this to the principal, then we shall
see. THEN WE SHALL SEE!"

Forgive me, father, but the principal's office was a little
living-room kind of place with big happy windows that
looked out on the day with little curtains and books in book-

shelves and little glass and copper and brass things all over stuck here and there, warm and cozy and bright. Little plants and soft chairs, a roll-top desk and a writing table with lamps and a rug and wonderful yellow polished wooden floors gleaming underneath. The principal didn't belong in this room. It was a good room, a human room. The principal didn't belong in this room or world or hemisphere. He belonged in the detention hall with a stick to beat you, where it was always dark and scary, where the most terrible unimaginable things were expected to happen. He came with terror but didn't belong anywhere, he couldn't have had a home or family. He only came out of the air of one bad time to the next, as though he dropped from heaven as the worst possible punishment and went back when you were reprieved. He had been dropped and lifted in and out of my life maybe twice before. Once for chewing gum and once for daring to wear a spotted, dirty pink check dress to school. His name was Mister Deans. He taught arithmetic. The bones in his cheeks hung out like cliffs with black eyes over them inside rotting holes. He was bald and tall and thin. He wore black suits and he hated. Children were the things he could vent it all upon, hitting them with rulers for making small mistakes in neatness, for smudge marks on a paper, for having your name on the left side instead of the right, up near the top. He was ominous and terrifying and monstrous but then so much of the world is like that when you're nine. Forgive me, father, for saying so.

I don't remember what he did to me for the pictures that I drew or if he did anything because while I was waiting for him in that room I confess I vomited and I was so afraid of having vomited, I confess I ran away. I didn't go back to school for days, hiding in the basement of my mother's house until everyone was gone to school or work or back to sleep, then creeping up the back stairs to the attic and waiting there, hungry and wretched with fear till three o'clock when

I would creep down again into the basement and out the cellar steps and in again through the back door, still afraid.

The violin teacher didn't understand why I didn't hold the violin correctly anymore, why I stared at him blankly when he asked me to take the bow in hand and begin my exercises and I couldn't. That it was over and I went blank and it meant nothing to me, more than nothing, it didn't exist and I could only stare at him. I couldn't make music. I couldn't stand the sound the strings made, it made me restless. The lessons were intolerable. His concern with detail was unfathomable to me. How could he care about all these dreary little scales? Didn't he understand that it was all meaningless, that nothing mattered somehow anymore and he wasn't real, dancing around and wailing at me as though the world was coming to an end. That none of it was real, only my daydreams.

There was a main street where I lived, that went from one railroad station to the next, and just along that street were all the shops and life and things to do, just there. There was a movie theater and a dress shop, a cleaner's, a car showroom, two delicatessens, little office buildings and a doctors' building and a candy store. Not much else. The old man in the candy store would hold the little paper bag while I pointed to the things I chose. A perfect square of dark, whitish, hard, stale fudge with shreds of coconut running through, a large malted chocolate ball, strings of long, thin, black, oily licorice and a peanut and molasses block wrapped in yellow paper. Five pennies and when I'd leave he'd begin to mutter, "Okay, get out, go on, get out, okay, get out, go on, get out," like a parrot. It seemed he never talked in any other way.

The janitor in the school building used to mutter, "Piss, shit, fuck, piss, shit, fuck, piss," while he pushed the broom and didn't look at anyone and didn't care who heard him muttering and we used to laugh at him behind our hands and whisper and stand where we could hear him say all the bad worst words there were, but we were always just a little scared of him and of the man who owned the candy store and of the muttering. It seemed so helpless and so dangerous and sad. What has to happen to a person to make him be this way, how many people have to leave him finally, so alone?

There were two old lady sisters who lived next door, on the right side if you faced the house, on the left if you were leaving. Two ugly thin and wrinkled spinster faces on top of black dresses and sensible shoes with little shriveled hands and necks who spent their lives watching and whispering. They kept cats.

"Tell us," they would say, "who was the man we saw going to see your mother last night? His car was parked in the driveway all night long. When we turned the lights out after twelve o'clock his car was still there. Your daddy is still away, isn't he? Your mother smokes cigars, doesn't she? Why wasn't she at the church bazaar? Does she teach you to say your prayers at night? Does she ask the dear Lord to take care of her little girl? Poor little girl, you must say your prayers every day and every night and ask the dear Lord to forgive you and your family all your sins. God have mercy on your little head. Who did you say the man was, dear?"

"He's my uncle," I lied to them. "He's my father's brother who comes to visit with my brother and tell us about our father in the war. My father's a hero, a general fighting in the war. My mother doesn't smoke cigars, she prays all day and all night for people like yourselves, dirty ugly people just like she said you were."

I confess there was a man whose car was parked there all night long, the man I told the neighbor ladies was my uncle. He brought a puppy dog to me, a little wiggly romping puppy dog all my very own, and over the fields and woods and days and nights we sailed together, the dog and I. But he wasn't my uncle, he was my mother's friend. He sat in the four o'clocks with her, with her hands in his, looking at her like he was reading words across her face that no one else could see but him, and all she saw was her own reflection in his eyes.

The dog would wait for me when I came home inside the front door and when he saw me he would go wild, running and wiggling and licking my arms and feet and shoes. Then he would turn and, not knowing what to do with himself, would bound up and down the stairs and when he got finished he would bound up and down them once again, then he'd come and stand by me and smile.

Upstairs in my room he would roll over on his back while I patted his stomach. I'd talk to him and tell him things that happened during the day. I confess I'd put my hand on his hairy little balls behind his cock and tickle them, his back legs would go like mad and I'd watch the red wet gooey thing come slipping out of its tan smooth shaft, a little red eraser, it looked like the top of a pencil. I confess I'd stroke his cock and he would start to shake and tremble still on his back, his legs would be going in all directions, that's when I would pull my panties off and let him smell my fingers that I was sticking inside myself and holding to his nose. The dog would jump up and come on me from behind, clasping my waist with his front paws and I became almost another dog for him while he banged and tried and pounded me in a wild frantic movement, whining and squealing and never losing the beat trying to fuck me and I'd keep myself moving around so he could reach me. I wanted him to reach me and touch me and get it in, but it never reached, no matter how I twisted myself it never reached.

"Come on dog, more," I'd yell at him, "more, come on, keep going," and I'd stick my finger back inside me, then hold it to his nose, and the weary, exhausted dog would strain and pant and start all over again, pounding my body and trying for something he couldn't find. It excited me how he pushed his body against me with that wet red thing crazy hungry, looking for its way. It made me wild to know how much he wanted it, how everything that lived wanted it, once they knew.

"Come on dog, FUCK."

The bedroom door flew open. My mother was standing there. She never said a word. She stood there watching what became a frozen anguish, endless torture time of me on the floor with my skirt above my waist and the pants beside me, with the dog on top clasping me and my legs apart for him, staring at my mother in the door. She turned, closed the door behind her, and was gone. At dinner that night I felt filthy and embarrassed. I sat with my head buried between my shoulders, picking at my food, not looking either way, little and caught, but she didn't say a word, no indication that anything peculiar or out of the ordinary had happened.

"Pass the butter, will you, dear. Thank you. Pass the bread. You're welcome. Time to do your lessons. Yes, you may be excused," and that was that.

The next day when I came home from school my mother told me that the dog was dead. She said he was poisoned by the neighbor ladies for tearing up their flowerbeds again this spring. It was from a piece of meat they threw to him, she said.

I confess I used to dash out between two parked cars and see the way the person who drove on the street jammed on the brakes and screamed and shouted at me, and I would be happy. That he really cared, that he didn't want to hit me or kill me, that my life mattered to him. I was grateful and I was warm inside from his concern. Whenever things got unreal for me I would stoop behind the cars and wait, and then I would dash and always the driver would slam on the brakes and swerve and shout at me. Sometimes they would get so angry they got out of the car and came storming over and grabbed me by the arm.

"You dumb kid, you almost got killed." And they would glare at me, holding me by the arm, hurting my arm. "Stupid kid, did you see how close you came to getting killed?" and he'd let me go and stand off, looking hard at me, and all I did was grin at him and feel marvelous because he gave a shit.

"Hey, father, do you give a shit?"

After I stopped playing the violin there was nothing to do. I couldn't do anything because I couldn't concentrate on anything but these vague dreams I had all the time I couldn't even name. I confess these were bad times for me. I did bad things and I was always afraid they would catch me and put me in jail and everyone would know about the bad things I was doing. Forgive me, father, for I have sinned.

At first I used to find myself going to stores very excited and when I got there I would steal little things, candy, pencils, rulers, thumbtacks, lipsticks, erasers, anything—it didn't matter, and I was alive again. That's how it began, it didn't bother me and I wasn't worried then. I was too excited about getting to the stores and pinching all these little things and getting home and putting them in a little cigar box I kept under my bed just for the things I pinched. It was marvelous filling the box up and then having to get another box and begin to fill it up again. I wasn't worried then. In the grocery store where the boxes of cold cereal were kept, I used to stealthily slink along the aisles and when no one was looking I opened the boxes and pinched out the little prize they always advertised on the radio or swiped the box tops for a contest they were having. And I was good. My fingers were fast and I never got caught and I filled maybe fifteen cigar boxes with the prizes and the box tops. I never entered the contests. I was only interested in the pinching. I mean my days and nights were beginning to matter again. As long as I didn't get caught I didn't care and I kept getting faster and better and collecting nails and bolts and wires from the hardware store, and candy from the five-and-ten, bottles of aspirin and chewing gum from the drugstore and all the box tops and gifts from the cold cereal in the grocery store. I even got the prizes out of Cracker Jacks and that was really skill, you never knew which side of the box the prize was at and if you had to turn the box over and fumble around, it would be easy to get caught. It would make a little, hard and stony noise and silence was the main thing.

That was my apprenticeship. It went on for maybe a year, two years maybe, until I was ready for bigger things like downtown. The stores in town became a kind of heady dizzy wonderland. The big move was from the five-and-tens into the department stores. At first I was so overwhelmed with the enormity of everything I didn't steal a thing. I just wandered in and out without thought, feeling my way, cooking up my system soon to come.

I would take a shopping bag, I thought, and whisk down aisles flipping things in, fast like a cat, big things now that were on the counter tops when there were people around, underpants and change purses, socks and hairbands, even once a pocketbook, even once a sweater. But my eye was really on the jewelry, trinkets were the most satisfying things to pick but also the most dangerous. Store people always had a kind of suspicion about jewelry, not good jewelry either, junk, but that was the best, the prize, the aim.

It was always on Saturdays when the city was bursting with people hurrying in and out of the stores with bundles and parcels, bumping into one another, mobbing, crowding, pushing. There were so many people, so many hordes of moving bodies that made one immense person pushing me to the table where the little trinkets were, the little junky jewelry all spread out on sale on little cardboard cards, glistening, calling, luring me to swipe them.

"Come on," they said, "over here."

I confess I was a pro by now. I had two years behind me of skill and involvement. I was ready for the dangerous luring tables full of junk.

Rings and bracelets, necklaces and earrings gold with little stones, rhinestones with fancy catches, fake emeralds and pearls, maybe even real cultured pearls set in ten-karat gold, inexpensive and insignificant but overwhelmingly enticing. I had money in my purse enough to buy twenty little pins or necklaces, but I had to pinch, I had to snatch, and I had to not get caught. This was the big league. Low-price stores on Saturday afternoons with trinkets all on sale spread out on tables begging to be pinched.

I inched my way up to the table and turned the cards over examining them as if I was making a decision for purchase, but all the time I was shooting looks around me to see who was watching me and who was suspicious. I understood suspicion, I understood the forbidden. It was my entire index. I understood it when my mother walked across a porch asking where he was, where was the boy. I understood what faces meant when they didn't say a word. I always understood the music all around me, the words were nothing. I decided on my choice. A little pin made of three circles of gold and in the middle was a pearl, maybe cultured, the card said it was. I put my hand on the pin and snapped it from the card and left my hand there a minute more. Then I put my fist around it like a vise and slowly, oh so infinitely slowly, I withdrew my hand with the pin inside from the table, looking casual and indifferent and even bored. I let my arm fall down to my side and slowly I began to walk away from the table. My heart was pounding in my throat, my cheeks were flushed, I could feel them getting hot, and I was gripped in exquisite panic as I headed for the revolving door through the maze of shoppers and bodies and smells, the carpeted floor between the aisles of things, and the noise and clutter. I had to get outside, outside I was safe, they couldn't pick you up outside, they weren't allowed.

But I never got to the door. A hand slammed down on my shoulder three steps away from the table. A terrifying hand smacked down on me and the music stopped. Almost dreamlike I reeled around and faced a horrifying, little, ugly, mean and sinister woman, smaller than myself, with a shoulder bag and hat and a tan suit, glaring, smileless, at me.

"Come with me." That was all she said and I went with her. All the people seemed to stop what they were doing to stare at us. In a dreamlike way they seemed to step aside while she guided me with her hand still on my shoulder to the back, and they made a path for us and stood back and stared at us, seeming to say, "Caught thief, caught, terrible thief, you're something worse than thief, what are you? You're caught," and they seemed to fade away and the store seemed empty and there was no music or sound or gravity as we floated to the back with her hand on my shoulder all in pale green shadows.

I was in a small dark room with filing cabinets, a window that had no shade, a light bulb coming from the ceiling, dingy, dark, and terrible. There was a man sitting behind the desk who stood up when we came in.

"Show him what you took. Go ahead show him." And she pushed me forward. I produced the pin. I started shaking. I put the tiny pin on the desk and tried to tell him I was sorry, that I didn't know what I was doing, that I could pay for it and poured out all the money I had in my purse all over his desk and asked him to take it, please to take it and to let me go. That he must not tell my mother.

"You're a child," he said to me, "about twelve years old."

"Yes, sir." He was a sad, kind man. He wasn't out for blood.

"Did you take a lot of things for a long time?"

"Yes, sir, but never from your store. I swear never from your store, and I never will again. Could I call my brother, please, he'll come for me, he'll take me home, and I'll never do it again. Can I call my brother?"

He handed me a piece of paper with words and lines on it and told me to sign my name. I was afraid. I looked at him.

"Go ahead," he said, "just sign your name, nothing will happen to you." I was too frightened not to and so I signed my name and that was the beginning of all the bad dreams and nightmares of being caught and found out by my parents and friends and teachers and the priest and the neighbor ladies and the man who owned the candy shop, and I was terrified.

"What are you looking for?" he asked me when he took the paper back. "What is it you really want that you have to do a thing like this? I've seen dozens like you, but I don't understand what you're looking for, what it is you're trying to get."

"I don't know," I said, "I don't know."

What was it, father, I was looking for, I never did find out.

I took the trolley home alone in a silence that lasted for days. There was no music playing for me anymore. I turned down the street and walked up my drive in silence, inside and out. I went to my room and sat there in a chair all the rest of the day. I didn't come down for dinner that night. Forgive me, father, but I told them I was sick and they all seemed to feel sorry for me, which made everything worse. As though they suddenly understood something was wrong and they were kind and spoke softly to me and offered me things which I couldn't take and they tiptoed out and smiled as they went and left me alone and frightened but better if I was alone. I prayed to Jesus but I could feel my prayers were not getting out, not being received, how could they? A thief can't pray, especially a thief who had been caught. I could do anything if I wasn't caught. I had no guilt or fear or worry but the instant I was caught I was paralyzed with fear and guilt and remorse. I thought badly of myself where before I never had. I felt worthless where before I felt superior for all my skill and cunning. Now I was a wretched thief in mortal fear of blackmail and prison and shame. Surely the paper they made me sign would be sent to someone, surely the next few days would tell it all, or maybe nothing would happen for a year, then one day a man would appear at the door and ask to see me and I would have to pay him a lot of money for the rest of my life. The store must run a little blackmail business on the side or why else would they make me sign that paper?

I confess it never happened, nothing ever happened to me and no one ever found out. I thought when we got married and it was announced in the papers, that they would come then from the store, then, I thought, would have been the perfect time to blackmail me, but even then it didn't happen. I never told another person about it but still at night when I'm just about to fall asleep there is this thing over there by the window, a big dark formless thing that only comes out when it's dark and seems to raise its arm and say, "Come on, come over here to me, come on, over here by the window," and I'm scared, father. It would always be standing over there by the window calling me, what is it, father? Over there by the window waiting for me, calling to me, what in God's name is it?

The Turtle never knew, he never saw it, instead he told me everything would be all right.

Forgive me, father, for I have sinned, I started sinning from the very beginning, I have always been sinning, I will continue to sin. When I was small I used to sit on the floor with a huge piece of string which I put knots into and I'd stuff the string inside my cunt, forgive me, father, but as I pulled the string out on every knot, I'd come, on every single one, and I confess I liked it. I liked it better than playing the violin, I really liked my piece of string. Forgive me, father, but there was a man on board who asked me for my underpants, to leave them in his stateroom, I didn't do that for him, forgive me, father, forgive me for being a little bit out of touch, forgive me for not being better. I should have done it, it was wrong of me to walk away from him, he asked me something understandable.

Forgive me, father, but I had a sister who killed herself, forgive me, I confess I didn't walk it off with her, I didn't see her suffering, I never helped her live, I should have, she was my sister. Forgive me for my mother's yellow lights that never saw, that never looked but only stopped where the noise was coming from. Was it all my fault? Yes of course it was all my fault. My father was never there, I don't know where he was but he was never there. Forgive me, father, for his never being there, forgive me for the man who came and sat with mother in the fading four o'clocks. I didn't mean it, I never meant to harm them, all of them, you have to understand I simply didn't realize how it would all turn out.

8

Art thrives on human suffering, not much else. That's when I started painting.

It was marvelous in the beginning, just like the violin was marvelous and stealing things was marvelous, so was painting. I painted swans out beside a creek with magic wings. I painted flowers and apples and grapes and cats. I painted my mother with her yellow eyes in yellow dresses and summer days and winter nights and stars and hills and streams and I painted a million pictures of myself and I painted my brother coming through a door, now this kind of door, now that, a hundred pictures of my brother and a hundred doors. I could have been a good painter if I stayed with it, I think, but once there was a girl I wanted to paint and when I couldn't paint her, then I quit.

I found her hitching a ride, no more than fifteen years old, full, with curly hair, sweet eyes, and courage, a knapsack on her back, with no commitment yet made to living. I picked her up and rode with her awhile, then I asked her if she would like to model for a painting, that I would like to paint her, and she was glad. She came every day after school wearing dungarees and a peasant blouse, little rings on every finger, and a sweeping smile that was remarkable. She had a harelip but you could hardly notice it, just a trace because surgery left it almost unnoticeable but the flaw itself was valuable, it made her more, it brought her forward, emphasized her, made her beautiful because it was part of her and she grew around it without bitterness and she soared. My brother would have loved her. She was just the kind of girl he would have loved. I almost loved her through his eyes. She was full, her hips were round and packed like her behind. She had large breasts and everything about her seemed contained with seams about to burst from her juicy plumpness. Sandals and dirty feet, authentic carelessness and unconcern and always with this flashing wild smile she must have found after they fixed her lip. She threw it at you and the world.

"Hey, look, my smile is beautiful now, isn't it?"

She was open for everything, ready and real. I wanted to paint the dreams she vaguely wore around her eyes, something about hitching cross country with a knapsack on her back, thumbing rides, not afraid. Something about becoming a potter and having babies with some boy somewhere who wouldn't mind a lot of things. I liked her. She was summer days and perspiration and oil. She was a breeze, a wildflower blooming near a rock. But I couldn't paint her, no matter how I tried I couldn't paint her. It just wouldn't happen. Always there was this stick figure fastened to the earth, nothing soaring, nothing moving, just this impossible gloom that kept coming on the canvas without life.

I thought that if the Turtle would fuck her I would have liked that. I really wanted him to fuck her, then I could have painted her, then it would have happened, but he only said hello and good-bye to her. He never stopped to give her breasts a feel, or kiss her smile. Why didn't he want to kiss that smile? Did he think I would have cared? I wouldn't have cared a bit. I would have understood. He only glared at me when I suggested it and walked away.

"Hey Turtle, fuck her."

"You're spooked," he said, "you're sick and wild and spooked. You fucked with dogs and stole things and you see things over by the window in the dark. You're all fucked up. How could you fuck with a dog? You're dirty and vile and disgusting. Did anyone ever tell you that?"

"You never went to college," the Turtle said. "You never got an education. Why didn't you ever get an education? Were you too fucked up?"

(My face flushes in shame.)

"You just sat there hibernating like a great bear waiting for thrills, that's all you ever did. Why didn't you ever go to college? Why did you steal things? What about your EDU-CATION?"

"Hey Turtle, you're going to make me cry. You're going too far."

"You're a thief," the Turtle said, "who never went to college."

Miss Sally killed her husband on a perfect summer night when the rose garden was in full bloom and the moon hung way up there in a periwinkle sky, completely yellow.

("Hey Turtle, I'm a writer now. No one can ever hurt me again. I'm saved.")

Then she cut his eyelids off with a fruit knife so his eyes would look forever without rest at eternity.

"What do you see?" Miss Sally asked him.

"But I'm dead," he said.

"Yes, I know," she answered him, "but tell me what you see."

"I see night birds flying to the moon, silver tears falling from their eyes."

"What else?"

"I see mothers who have truly understood their children."

"Yes, what else?"

"I see nothing else."

"What do you feel?" Miss Sally asked her husband.

"But I am dead," he said.

"Yes," she answered him, "I know, but tell me what you feel."

"I feel freedom. There is no bondage anymore. There is no dependence or need. Yes, death is total freedom. It doesn't care."

"Will you come back to me?" Miss Sally asked her husband.

"No," he told her, "for I am dead."

I'm writing, Turtle, I'm really writing well these days, and if that's all that I can do, then I'll do it right. Maybe it's the only peace I'll ever find and if it's the only peace that I can ever find, I'll find it here, right here with words across a bit of paper. But the Turtle didn't hear.

He became a phantom who came and went. We were gone so far apart. The Turtle couldn't touch me where I was, not anymore. Now there were two children who didn't enter where I lived, not even them, not now. They played around me making bigger circles and farther borders that I couldn't reach. Their voices shattered me. Their demands diminished me and I ran from them.

And I was losing people. I could feel the human thing drift away from me. It was like a dream I kept having night after night all in washed-out greens, almost smoky greens in a woods early in the morning. A girl in chiffon with bare feet playing blindman's buff with a drape around her eyes so she couldn't see, twirling with her arms out to reach but the people in the circle were going farther and farther back from her, tiptoeing backwards away from her.

"Where are you?" she would say. And they all whispered, "Sh-h-h-h, sh-h-h-h," and tiptoed farther and farther back, away from where she was and when she pulled the blindfold off they were gone and she was alone in bare feet and chiffon, lost in the woods that were smoky green.

Then a boy came out of all of it, barefoot and wearing

chiffon just like her—lost like she was lost—and they clasped hands and danced round and round playing childish games and laughing and dancing and holding hands.

But that was just the dream, you see. I wasn't saved, over in the corner it still was there. As soon as the lights were off the thing was there, big and dark and formless. I would lie on my back rigid next to the sleeping Turtle, afraid to look at it. It's only in your mind, I would say, it isn't real, and I'd shoot a fast look at it and there it was, big and dark and formless, calling me with one arm reaching, beckoning me to the window and far down below was the street.

Come on, it said, come over here, come on.

It's only in your mind, I kept on telling myself and I'd shoot up and flick the lights on and it was gone.

"Hey, Turtle, it was there, it was there again when the lights were off. It was there again."

And the Turtle looked but he said he didn't see it. He said that it was only in my mind but I couldn't turn the lights out after that, the Turtle did when I was finally asleep.

9

My brother wrote his first play for a Christmas Eve when we were small. The house was filled with green and silver bells and stockings, gifts wrapped in colored paper. That's when he wrote the first play for my sister, himself, and me, to be given after all the gifts were exchanged and opened, when the family was all together in the little room with all the books that was the only room that stormed with life and disorder and movement in that silent, drafty old Victorian house.

While we said our lines staring off into space, not looking right or left, he hummed and made all kinds of noise effects —thunder, wind, clapping, train whistles—in the background until it was time for him to deliver his line with total commitment. The play was crucially important to him, and his plays were good and they praised his plays and every Christmas time he had another little play for the three of us, each year more elaborate, each year more complex and different, getting hard to understand, getting muted but showing early signs of something good and sensitive. He was good, he knew that he was good, they knew that he was good and they praised him. Each year we became more and more alive in the little play, each year earlier and earlier in the season we started preparing for them, getting costumes ready, making stage sets, more elaborate plans, lighting, and he wrote more and more for us to memorize, worked us harder and harder and we were better and better. Each year my father brought people in. It was the only time I can remember my father being there, bringing people in, being happy and proud, being part of the house. There were card chairs delivered and punch made and we had our play. Each year the plays got longer and then one year there was in the sun porch off the dining room a rod extended and a curtain with pull strings and a footlight; he had his theater. There was nothing greater for all of us.

"Such talented marvelous children," they would all say, "such extraordinary talented children."

"Yes," my mother said, "we are very special people."

But it was his production that was marvelous, it was my brother who brought the life and meaning into a drafty old Victorian house essentially for his own pleasure. He had a way of making things crackle around him with life, he could make things happen when he was bored enough. He could write clever things, interesting things, things that made you wonder what would happen next, and in the end it was always startling, made people, even grown-up people, somehow catch their breath, then a pause and then a sigh and lots of clapping, and he loved it. He would stand there watching all the faces looking at him, reading the faces, studying the faces, smiling but intense.

There was always an enormous letdown when the play was given and done for that year. We couldn't find ourselves or our meaning in that house for days after the play was done. We wandered, bad-tempered at each other. All the months of arranging and sewing and fixing and preparing, and after the play was over we were filled with gloom as we took things apart and put them away for another year. He was the most withdrawn of all.

It was on a Christmas morning years after the last play was

ever given that they found my sister dead on the kitchen floor, twenty-five sleeping pills and half a bottle of bourbon pumped into her, dead. . . .

"Such talented children, such marvelous talented children," that's what all the people said who came and watched us and now the marvelous children were all free-falling in the night. She was dead. I was grabbing onto bits and snatches of what I could, going farther and farther out to sea, running from something I couldn't even name, and she was dead.

What was it over there when the lights went out, looming near the window in the dark, that frightened me? This destructive blob of fearsome thing standing always over there in the dark that I had to keep running from? What was it? Who was it? What did it want from me? Who would grab me from it next and keep me while I waited till it went away, till I wasn't scared so bad? Who could fill me up and save me from it for just a little while till it went away?

"Who was that man I saw you with?"

"What man?"

"You know what man."

"Oh, that man, just a man out beside the creek who fed the ducks in the park, it was such a hot day. I didn't know where to put myself so I went to the park, I never said a word to him, just stood there watching him feed the ducks, I just stood there watching him. I don't know who he was, he never said a word to me."

The Turtle turned away.

"The marvelous children all free-falling in the night to the very bottom. The Christmas plays were wonderful, weren't they, old Turtle man, do you remember when things used to really taste good, when the snow fell silently and made the world a magic cream puff filled with every kind of possibility? Do you remember all that, old Turtle man, was it ever so glorious for you when you were small?"

"No," he said, "it was always real, even when I was small, it was always real."

Oh, but not for us, old Turtle man, it was wonderful at Christmas time, the way he arranged it all and the way we worked. My father brought in all the friends he had and made a great wassail, the house was warm and filled with lovely things that always seemed to show up and come alive at Christmas time, you never noticed them all the rest of the year. The chairs and paintings and tables and the little things on table tops, only at Christmas time they showed like that. The way the house smelled with sweet things coming from the corners and lifting to the top of everywhere. There were always presents wrapped in silver paper with ribbons, and the snow would blanket all of it with something pure and new and clean and silent, and hide the traces of the past, and who could imagine a future, only now, here, when we all were happy for just a little while when the logs were burning in the fireplace and the smoke would lift out of the chimney to the winter afternoon. I could see the smoke rising to the sky. I could have almost grabbed it then if I needed to, it didn't go too fast when I was young.

But now the night was a black horse with a black rider galloping in to terrorize me, the night closed in on me like a curse. Nothing mattered. I didn't care anymore, slowly caring had drifted away from me and there was nothing that mattered, nothing at all. Life became a night train going backwards into hell, the last stop—apathy. The marvelous children, free-falling in the night, and far down below was the street.

I didn't get out of bed in the morning, I lay there half awake, not moving, staring. I didn't answer the telephone, I didn't greet people who came, I didn't need them, they couldn't help me get out of bed and comb my hair or brush my teeth. They were weighing too heavy on the marrow of my bones, all of them. My face began to get all green and thin and sallow all the time and I didn't care. My body was slipping away to almost nothing from not eating. How to eat when everything looked like the soles of shoes, everything tasted like the soles of shoes? Afraid of food poisoning, afraid I would choke on a fish bone, easier not to eat at all, stopped eating. Not sleeping, reaching in the dark for little pills and waiting to fall asleep, but they didn't always work and when they didn't, that thing over there beside the window, the fearsome terrifying shadowy thing, would get bigger and I would watch it.

Who are you, I would shout at it, who the hell are you and what do you want? Are you death? Are you the same monster who handed my sister the sleeping pills? I would start to sob and shake and cry until the Turtle sat up next to me, flicking on the light and telling me it would all be all right. What would be all right? He didn't know, but he promised me it would.

"Do you see it over there, Turtle? Can you see it when the lights are out, the damned lousy rotten thing, it's only when the lights are out. It's destroying me."

Why didn't my brother write, why doesn't he ever answer the letters I send to him?

The Turtle gathered my bones in a laundry bag and began the trip with me from one great doctor to the next. Nothing was there, nothing was found. Nerves they told us, emotional upset, fatigue, and nerves, nothing to worry about, only nerves. The Turtle stopped what he was doing, all his comings and goings ended and he dedicated himself to me. He worried about me to begin with. His face was still and white while he watched me running from one room to the next and gasping for my breath. He brought me soup and orange juice and took me to another doctor, and still another one, but all they said was nerves. He loved me best when I was sick. It didn't matter much what was wrong with me as long as I was sick and broken and weak. He found me most attractive then when I was limp and asked nothing of him but only thanked him gratefully for any kindness he could give. It was a thing with us. When I was well I bounded around him, in and out of his life, and brought a kind of strength that he found frightening. When I was sick I was easy to be with. He could gather my bones and carry them wherever he wanted and he was good to me when I was sick. He seemed happy when I was sick, interested and involved and cheerful. The first time it happened we were in a hotel room that looked over the whole of the city just before dawn. He was sleeping in a bed across from me, I stood by the window terrified, something in me was saying to jump, to end it all and jump into the street that was down there calling up to me. Come on, it said, come on, do it, do it.

"Get up," I screamed at him, "get up and walk with me, let's get out of here! Walk with me."

He staggered from his sleep and threw some clothes on and walked with me.

"Did it ever happen with you like this?" I asked him. He said it did. I didn't want to die. I really didn't want to die, it wasn't that I loved life so much, I just had too many fantasies yet that weren't lived, and that's what made the difference.

Yes, he said he understood, but I didn't love him. Then I began to realize I didn't love him, I didn't love anyone and that was death.

10

In the beginning I was too sick.

Spinning days in and out of sleep and anguish. Shades of daylight and lamplight noises quiet and muffled, fading away into sleep brought by shots in my arms and legs, shots in my behind, anguish, legs in white stockings coming and going away. Pills and needles and anguish. When I would open my eyes there was a kind face looking down at me and then it would fade away, smiling eyes grooved in deep lines around the smiling eyes and then it faded away from me. I tried to hold on to the eyes but I couldn't, I drifted too far away. I lost it all in smells and sweating and floating, lost in a sea of anguish. Days without weather or time. Days without daytime or nighttime, days without time, in and out of anguish or sleep or shots until the noises became more real, until the room became more white with a table and a window and a window shade, a curtain. There was a curtain there. There was a bed under me. The legs were parts of people coming in and leaving and when I heard the noises they were real and the anguish was less and the face was there when I looked again. There was a man standing beside my bed looking down at me and smiling. My eyes could see him. I felt the boiling tears fill up and silently begin to drop over, one by one. I could see the man and feel his warmth and kindness and I was real again.

"You've been sick," he said, "you've been very sick but you're going to be better. You've had a very hard time, but you're going to be better. You're back now. You're here again. You were away, but you're back now and you're going to be better."

The child floating in the garden staring at her fingers, her hair caught on the breeze, pulls her skirts away and stares at her fingers. The child drifting on the summer of new yellow grass and lace leaves flecked with pinks and reds marked with evergreens to make a frame around the dream. The child floating in the cobwebs of illusion, a virgin flower once again blooming hope inside the rambling walls. The marmalade moisture people smiling with their cherry cheeks and fatness, shabby shoes and looseness in the timeless garden, yellow lace spring where the grass and budding trees met each other in velvet blooming wood out here where the world crept away without a knock. Peace and space and healing. Nothing could enter this sanctuary of healing out here where the world crept away. No morning papers anymore, no mail or telephones to break the stillness, it was empty without loneliness, filled with peace and time to lick the wounds and pat the darkened area and heal out here where he would come each morning and sit with me and try to find the secrets without judgment. Something understanding, he accepted everything without surprise where there was no holding back, where nothing was a surprise and truth was decent, it was all right to be truthful. What a gift, what a scary gift.

His hair was light, straight hair that fell across his eyes. He was thin and full of lines, grooves that made a map across his face. He belonged to himself, couldn't be whipped into anything, couldn't be forced. He was light. He was weightless. In his quietness he was light and easy to carry and in his lightness he could carry all of us. I used to wait for him in a kind of breathlessness, aware of the smallness I had become, aware of the wispy airlight creature that was floundering in the breeze. I felt minute. I used to wait for him wondering, wondering about the first days of my life, feeling them again and being tied into all my days. He was the common denominator of my time. I was in pain waiting for him, an intense and bulging set of moments until I saw him walking up the hill and toward me. Smiling wide. The Doctor-smile.

I didn't hear the wailing then, when I was there, the death echo over everything was in the seashell. There was no death then. There was no illness or sorrow, there was no aching understanding for each creature's scant and terrified time, his and hers and ours and mine and theirs, all of theirs. No matter how they said it didn't bother them, it did. Those awful moments were gone when you suddenly realized the worst of all of it was Nothing. The endless nothing that you're headlong rushing into when you feel the quicksand of eternity and hear its wailing. I was scared of death and I was courting it. I was terrified of dying, dancing all in feathers round and round it, begging to be tagged.

It was incredibly beautiful out my window where the crimson magnolias were almost ready to open their wondrous fists into full bloom dotting the blue-black spruce trees with spring. A yellow lace spring with everything in brandnew bud and just beginning again. The spring. The oak trees and the willow trees dancing their variations beside each other, one silky falling down next to strength and majesty, branches looped in a spring dance. I thought of the children and how they saw the spring without me there this year. If the little girl still held her breath when she fell asleep at night and stared almost in hypnotic trance before she finally closed her eyes as she did when she was on the breast. Her sleep-time breathing was still as it was when she was on the breast, the little girl with the golden hair all falling in her eyes. I needed her but they didn't bring her to me. Why wouldn't they bring her to me? Not now, they said, not now but later. So I made gifts for the doctor, for the Smile that came over the top of the hill each morning and sat with me. I touched his hand and told him of the children and he listened. I was away now, but I'd be back, he said, one someday I would be back watching them chase the swan at my mother's house, giving it bits and crumbs and laughing, and I'd answer them when they called, I would be there to answer them, not to turn my blind lights to the spot where the sound was coming from and not be able to hear.

The great magician with his emerald velvet cloak was smiling at me under the willow trees with the gray mist hanging in like a blanket where I could hide while I sat there smiling and watching him. He kept dancing before me twirling his great emerald velvet cape round and round. Wait for me, I would shout, wait, wait, I'm coming too. Then I would leap over the little foot rocks and he would follow me trying to find me and catch me but I was gone, too fast, too fast, I was gone again. Can you find me, I would beg him, whispering, dancing, whirling out along the beaches by the sea, hear the music coming from the horizon, feel the stars talking jibbering gossiping about all of it, hear them. They are wicked jealous peeping stars to watch me, that's all they have to do just watch me trying to catch something. I'm going to catch it and not let go, help me, help me. I am healing? The stars feel like ice and the nuns across the beach are holding balloons tight by the strings. Not for Sale. They're not for sale tonight. Just hold them there, stand on the beach, holding the balloons, while I dance by, reaching for more stars. I'm high, high, high, flying into the stars headlong, not being able to stop flying into the stars, can't catch me now, can't catch me anywhere.

I'm smearing paint across the canvas. The Smile told me to paint again or maybe write if I was ready, but first I had to do the girl and give her to my brother, then I'd write for all the rest of time.

Dashing color with something free and flying, darting around and sloshing more and more. The girl's face appears in the clouds up near a sun that is laughing, roaring with laughter, the girl with the full breasts and rings on every finger, the happy, full-hipped, juicy girl is coming out of the sky and the dreams all across her eyes, hitching cross-country and finding something. Finding something precious is happening, the great painting is happening, and I can't stop it all from happening all by itself. And the Smile sits with me and watches. Coffee and speeding into more and more reds and yellows are coming into the corners, no sketches, no time, no stopping. Flying into orange, greens, and wild purples coming over the other side, sending the whole thing into something that is flying and dancing all at once in roaring laughter from the sun up at the top, and the smiling harelip girl bursting out of her clothes and skin and dreams. I can paint the girl!

"Your brother's here to see you."

Tell him to go away. Tell him I don't want to see him. Tell him I'm painting him a woman he can have. Tell him all he can do with real women is destroy them. Tell him he never answered the letters I used to write him, the long letters, five, maybe seven pages about my life, what was happening to me, about the dark thing in the corner. Tell him how he changed, how success ruined him and made him too fancy for ordinary people. How he forgot people who he used to owe a lot to, people like my mother and myself. Tell him how he only always cared about his fucking self. Tell him that, then see if he'll stay, if he still will want to talk to me. Tell him how I almost died, and if I had died he never would have seen me again. Ask him if he would have cared.

Did he need me anymore, ask him that. No, I'll bet he tells you he doesn't need anyone, not anymore, not even ME. I bet he tells you that. Go ahead and ask him. He's a big shot now.

Remind him of my fourteenth birthday coming in from away. Remind him that he wore a bandage around his head and he was embarrassed to look at me again and tell him how it hurt me to see him not able to look at me, not in command anymore, ashamed. Tell him that, see what he says when he finds out I've talked about it all. See if he remembers that my grandmother was coming but still the boredom when I was with him edged disaster, tell him that. Tell him how restless and tearing and frantic the boredom was when he pinned me there, it was monstrous, tell him that, go ahead. See what he says. See if it undoes him.

He used to take the neighbor's cat up on our third floor, open the window and throw the cat clear into their garden. It was an enormous heave and I would scream and cry and bite his arm and shout at him and he would laugh, my God, how he would laugh. The cat would land and lie there looking dead, it didn't move for minutes and I was sure that it was dead, but slowly it picked itself up and hobbled, dazed, bumping into trees and falling down again. I ran down the steps and out to the cat and picked it up. It scared me. Anything that was sick or dying scared me. But I picked it up and took it to the little old sisters and I told them that the cat was run over by a car. The little old freaks shouted and cried and called the vet and in a day or two the cat was outside again and I was afraid for the cat. Go tell him how I hated him for doing that, how much I hated him. Then see if he'll want to come in and see me. See if he's ashamed.

He used to take me down in the basement and stick cigarettes in my mouth. He made me light them and inhale them while he leaned against the furnace acting like a grown-up, puffing away.

"Now," he says, "if you tell Mother, I'll tell her you were

smoking too." The room got dizzy. I fainted and he ran away.

Once he was throwing apples at the passing cars and he gave the apples to me and I threw too. One car stopped. The man got out and chased him. I stood there and the man caught me. I lied, said I didn't know the boy, and he came out from hiding when the man was gone, laughing, oh God, how he was laughing. Tell him that, tell him how he stuck me all the time and how I've always paid and protected him besides.

Remind him how he was walking on the stone wall and I was walking on the pavement and how I put my hand on the wall in front of him, not thinking, and how he stepped on my fingers, how he mashed my fingers under him, ask him why he did it, I'd really like to know. Things like that always came as a surprise.

My mother always got dressed up for him when he came home from boarding school. I used to wonder why she went all-out with special scarves and special makeup and special nail polish just because he was coming home, after all, he was her son, but she did and I thought it was peculiar, just like she did for her friend who always came at four o'clock, the one who stared at her all the time. It was curious, the whole thing was always curious. She always smiled to herself, little mysterious smiles, and put perfume on and kept on smiling to herself. She was a group of people all in one with a little something of death there, fey, that's the word, in touch with the other world all round her eyes. She understood him, they understood each other, but no one ever understood about me. Tell him that, tell him all of that and see if he still wants to come in and see me, visit with me now when I'm like this, here in this place, broken and wild and miserable, see if he's brave enough, if he is up to it, go ahead and tell him. Remind him about the cat, go ahead, remind him. Tell him that's when the road for me suddenly began inward and silent.

Masked people began to dance behind their smiling plumage of pretending. Nothing was real. I watched them dancing all round their kind of denials and omissions, round their dreams and aspirations, round their failures and their fantasies. Nothing was real. There was no kernel that anyone could offer to the other, there was no strong, there was no constant, there was no beat, it all was jerky dancing to a tinny little song that didn't matter.

My father? My father was never there. Never there.

Once I saw him lean against a tree outside the house. He leaned against his arm and cried. How many years ago was it when he cried into his arm and I was standing beside him and waiting? He looked down at me and pulled me to him and hugged me, a long long time he held me close to his legs out beside the trees and then he walked back to the house holding my hand and whimpering, tears streaming down his cheeks. He was not remote, my father, but he went away, I don't remember him ever being there.

"Shall I tell your brother to come in now?" he asks me.

"Yes."

I I

The first five minutes were all there were of recognition, of past, of love, of something warm, of reunion. And then attaching oneself to conversation.

I was making the accounting as I spoke with false enthusiasm and unreal gaiety. I was watching his slenderness and sunken eyes, his shoulders hunching a little bit, his head still as always hung low, not really facing me, looking down at his feet, rubbing his hair with his other hand, scratching his head. The same first few minutes. The same avoidance. The same embarrassment and shame until he was in command again.

"It was hard for you to come here," I told him, "but I'm glad you came."

"How did you get yourself so fucked up?" he asked me. "What happened?"

"It just happened," I told him, "I didn't have to really try."

"You were always fucked up," he told me.

"Does it run in families?" I asked him.

The first five minutes were all there were. The first few looks that rock you back to a certain thing that isn't anymore, to a time that is remote. It's gone away but there are echoes, faint tiny echoes still that you can hear, of course you still can hear them, but they are only echoes now. Now he's a strange country I can't find on the map. He's a Christmas card from nice people I used to know whose home I was once invited to, that remote, that echoey, that out of reach but with something, some little something still not altogether gone away. Echoes. Something curious that keeps you wondering over and over again about him, and when you see him standing there and breathing and doing and bragging and scared and human and real, it's done almost in a glance because there is nothing anymore to be shared. That's what kills a lot of it, the nothing anymore that you can share.

I never had a brother, I had a lover. I never knew what the word "brother" could mean, what the word "sister" could mean, what the word "mother" could mean—it was all meaningless to me, all except what it felt like being with him, that was the only meaning.

"Listen, about your writing plays," he begins, "I read what you sent me about the gal who killed her husband. It stinks. You were good at the violin, why don't you go back to it? You did nice paintings, why don't you stick to that? Don't fuck around with a typewriter, you're a bomb. I've started writing my first play since we were kids, something I've always wanted to do. When I'm finished with it I'll take you anywhere you want to go when you get out of here, we'll just take off. Just get better, then we'll take off. How 'bout it?"

My brother goes over to the Smile to shake his hand, doesn't look at him, keeps his head down and whips out his hand like a toy gun, still close to his body, almost in a comical theatrical way, but the Smile only looks at him without moving.

"Why don't you try to help her?" the Smile asks.

My brother doesn't answer. Only his body jerks into one large human fist.

"She's a fucking idiot, that's what she is," and he reels around, pointing a finger right into my nose and pressing it.

His face is red, his shoulders are rounded as though he is going to hurl himself at me and then explode.

"My little sister, my little sister, ask her why she hates me so much. Ask her why she had to always keep on trying to outdo me. But I won't let her, I'll never let her. Tell her to keep her fucking hands off a typewriter. The theater is going to be mine. That's mine, do you hear me, little sister, that is mine and I'm not going to give it to you. All my life since the day you were born, since the day they brought you home, loud and crying and eating everything in sight that was mine, that belonged to me, I gave things to you, shared everything I had with you or else you took it, you just took what you wanted and walked away happy. But not plays."

He turns back to the shrink, his finger still on my nose.

"We used to get report cards on the same day. She always got good report cards. Mine were lousy. They praised her. They turned ice on me. All good marks, all good comments, everything she did was good until she got all fucked up. Then hers were as bad as mine. She played the violin, she was good, got a prize, got a lot of fuss until she didn't give a shit anymore. Then she started painting. She was good at that too, she could really paint, I mean like it mattered to her, but then something else happened—who knows what—and she quit that too. She always understood things nobody else understood. She always said things that made a lot of sense. I never knew anyone like her, never. I tried to find it in a million girls, but they never had what she had, none of them, she was different. It was easy for her. She was cool and quick and smooth and it all came easy for her. She never seemed to try. It just came out of her. The rest of us were knocking ourselves out, but she just sat there and there it always was. She was fucking around since she was nine or ten, did she ever tell you that? Did she ever tell you how she did it with my best friend once in my bed? He told me. He told me the next day. 'Your sister,' he said, 'she's a hot one.' I tried to kill him. The little whore, did she ever tell you that?

They should have locked her up in here years ago, kept her off the street that way."

He takes his finger off my nose. I feel the blood creep slowly back into my face as if it were patiently waiting at the front door for its turn, not in a hurry.

"I used to write Christmas plays every year, we had another sister, the three of us put on my plays, but the plays were mine, every bit of them, and they were good.

"I've built seventeen buildings. I've built eighty-three fountains, eighty-three, and I like my fountains and I like my buildings and I'm going to write my play—not her. She's not the only one who lives, you know. Tell her that. Tell her to keep her dirty hands off a typewriter."

He swings around and faces me again, his face is wet with tears.

"And tell her to keep out of my bedroom," he says to me. "Do you hear, tell the little whore to keep out of my bedroom!

"You're all fucked up," he says. "Don't give advice. Just take it. Go back to playing the violin. Paint a little picture of a swan. Do what you can do. That's what's real, what you can do, and what's insane is trying to do what you can't. No plays, remember? I will not allow you to—do you understand?"

"One thing I have to tell you before you go, just one thing," I said to him.

"What is it?"

"You're the whore, not me."

My brother got that angry look on his face again but I didn't stop, not this one time. I kept on talking, afraid of him but it didn't stop me.

"You're the whore because you're the one who sold out for money and lost your truth. I never did. There was no truth in anything you've done, no love, no message, no art, no fidelity to the dream. All you've done were ugly buildings in ugly cities and ugly fountains that made me ashamed. I wouldn't believe it at first, but that's all they were, ugly and ordinary and terrible. You copied other people. You felt nothing, you pretended, like a whore, all for money. You picked other people's styles and matched other people's ideas and put it up on some corner with some crappy animal spouting water. There was nothing ever there that was your own except the Christmas plays you used to do when we were kids.

"When it got easy for me I quit. When there wasn't any dream or search I began again somewhere else trying to find something all my own and my own way of saying it and giving it. I was always faithful to the dream, to the search, everybody's search that they try to forget, that they bury under the everyday heartache of a dreamless world they live in, looking to forget. But I couldn't forget, that was my job, not to forget. To remember the overwhelming struggles and the fractured dream and keep them and understand another kind of truth, and put them all together and call it art. Not to abandon the dream and the struggling restlessness and the truth, no matter what anyone else would call it, there was truth in all the chaos and the suffering that I had to give. You called me an all-fucked-up whore because I made love with your best friend in your bed. What's that got to do with being real? Tell me that. What's it got a single thing to do with being real?

"You're all fucked up," he says. "That's why you're here in a hospital. You were always fucked up. Just get better, just see things the way they are, the way they really are. That's enough of a job for you. Just paint those swans or the little harelip girl and stop trying to stretch yourself farther than you can reach. Don't compete with me for all your life. It doesn't pay. But then I don't care, it's your life, it's up to you."

His marriage was over, another marriage was over, done

and finished. His wife picked up and left and took the child with her. She got fat again and she started drinking. He didn't want me to write. That's why he was here.

"Does it run in families?" I asked him again. "I mean about the twenty-five sleeping pills. Do you think it runs in families?"

"Don't be an idiot," he said, "you'll be all right."

The little red-headed bird flew into the wind. She flew with the girl, a friend of hers, that's who she really flew with. She loved the girl, the friend. My mother said she loved her best of all, better than her husband, better than her family, this girl, this one she flew with all the way and couldn't find a way back.

They were childhood friends, grew up holding hands and telling secrets, giggling and whispering, my sister and that girl. She was married but it didn't stop between them, the closeness, the whispering, the telling secrets. They took trips together, went away together, came back together, left and returned, fought and cried and sulked and made up. Always this was the closeness for the little red-headed bird, always with her head in that girl's lap with the girl stroking the red mop of ringlets, always the sharing. The friend went away. The letters came that she wasn't coming back, they were young, both of them were young still, and pretty and full and funny, both of them, but after the girl went away, my sister roamed aimlessly. I remember her roaming around as if she were dazed, foreign, far away. She came back to my mother's house at Christmas time that year and sat in a chair silently, still, gazing, not talking. My mother badgered her, questioned her, strained her, but she never answered, she just sat there aimlessly, and when she walked with me she talked aimless, roaming talk that made no sense.

And she'd laugh. She would laugh and laugh and then

she'd heave enormous sighs and stare off into space. She needed help but she didn't get it. No one knew she needed help. No one ever heard her.

My mother said it was a heart attack when they found her on the floor with twenty-five sleeping pills and half a bottle of bourbon floating in her bloodstream. Dreadful heart attack, runs in the family, bad hearts. Terrible, terrible, and my mother closed up like a clam and kept wringing her hands together.

"A heart attack, Mother?" I asked her. The drawer was closed again and when you opened it that instant later, everything that was put in there was gone.

"You mustn't mention her to me, not now or ever, never to mention her name to my face. Terrible thing, a disgrace to all of us, she's disgraced us all and I can't forgive her. I can't forgive her. Do you understand me?"

"Yes."

"Bad hearts run in the family. You shouldn't smoke. She smoked too many cigarettes, you should take better care than she did. Do you understand?"

"Yes."

She started humming that eerie high-pitched little melody and smoothed her hair, walking around the room, the drafty, empty, old and fading room, with a shawl wrapped around her shoulders.

"I'll never forgive her, do you hear me? I'll never forgive or understand her. To hurt me so, to ruin my life, I don't know what I did to deserve such a thing. I gave her everything she ever wanted, everything. I'll never understand it, what I did to deserve such a thing. I had an aunt who did it, maybe it just runs in families, maybe that's the only explanation."

"This ship isn't going anywhere," I tell the great smiling face that comes over the hill, "absolutely nowhere, it has nowhere to go, it's just on a trip, that's all, with nowhere to go. I don't understand this perplexity. You had better give me a reason for all of this no-destination business."

"There isn't any reason, there isn't any destination that's all, not here, that's the rule. Just in and out and around but nowhere special, you can leave at the next port, if there is one, we never know."

"But I have places to go and things to get tended if you don't mind. I'm sorry but I can't stay forever here."

"You can't get off immediately," he smiles at me like a great expanding Cheshire cat until the smile is hanging out the limits of his face, hanging in the daytime, just centered in his face, this huge smile extending past his cheeks just hanging in the sunshine, hung on right under his nose.

"You must wait till we get somewhere, anywhere, unless of course you're prepared to drift or drown."

"This is preposterous."

"Is it? We advertised it as the cruiseless cruise, the spontaneous assault on the water, the real grasp of leisure. (It isn't important that they call it madness, it's not madness, it's the real grasp of leisure.) If you didn't want all that, you might have taken another tour, a bus company or an airplane. But everybody here doesn't mind. They are all just sitting there and not mingling at all, they have no needs, no desire, no concern, they are relaxing."

"Are you quite certain we're not going anywhere at all? Are you positive?" I asked him again.

"Yes, I'm certain we aren't going in any direction. We will probably find something though, it's the usual way, we will eventually come across something because we are circling round and round in bigger and then smaller circles, sometimes huge ones, sometimes tiny little ones, but there are gulls, and you must know that whenever there are gulls, something's close at hand, a place to stop and settle for a day perhaps, maybe even three days, gulls are always the first indication. Whatever we come across, however, will be a surprise to all of us. Maybe it will be worthwhile, maybe not, maybe it will be a disaster, maybe salvation, who's to know, who can say, not even after it's done. No one really to tell you if it was worthwhile or not, only you can decide that, and then you can tell us all at tea if you care to, and if you don't, then be still."

"I'm going to have a tantrum," I told him, "that's what's required to put direction into all these strange things you're saying, I am going to have a very serious tantrum."

"Go right ahead," he said, "your tantrum is the highest power of leisure, it will be charming afternoon entertainment. It's your tantrum and if you're willing to display it, go ahead, but no one will share it with you."

"I think I should leave the ship immediately, over the railing and out of sight under the oily indifferent mother sea, a fine meal for the sharks tonight that hadn't planned on something as nice as me, not even in their wildest moments.

"Someone is kissing my leg," I tell him, "without a doubt there is someone creeping up behind me, kissing my leg."

"It's very possible," he says.

"But you must tell him to stop, he's licking it and stroking it and kissing it. For God's sake, he's unusual, he's inspired.

"Hold on, brother, I'm not sure I'm ready for all that, you're going too fast down there, you're falling in love with it, and I'm not sure I want all of that, just a little would be one thing, yes, but all of it, the letters and sonnets and gifts, I'm not quite certain."

"Too late," he moans. "Too late, I'm in love, I'm in love, never such a leg before, it's entering into me to where I live and breathe and see and feel and hear. All of me is flooded with your divine leg, what can I do for it, what can I get for it, how can I immortalize it forever?"

"Hold on there, I'm not sure yet, I'm really not, it likes you a little, it responds with a smile and a blush, tell me more, make me cold and hot and nervous, make my heart beat and make me want to rush all around in circles, frantic.

Hurry, I have to know, do you want it? How much do you love it?"

"I love it now, I might not love it later, I might not want it later, but I want it now. But then later doesn't matter, does it?" He looks up at me from the floor, bewildered.

"No," I tell him, "later doesn't matter really.

"You can have it then," I tell him, "for all the rest of time it's yours. It's not mine anymore, it belongs to you."

He is weeping on the floor, sobbing in a heap of happiness —and real—and I promise him I will change completely from now on. I'll be someone else, I think, it's time to be someone else, caring about different things, things that didn't matter before, they will matter now, all new, different things will become important.

Letters addressed to my leg started arriving on rice paper, little trinkets, scarves and love beads, incense until he went away. He fell asleep on a deck chair out there in the sun and my leg slipped away from him, he let it slip, I suppose. Gone to nothing, to absolutely nothing, only have a leg left to remember him by. All the rest of me is dust. Fleeting, fleeting, I detest growing older, watching things go ugly and loose. It didn't matter where the ship was going, he told me, it wasn't the essential feature of the cruise, the thing that really mattered was the trip itself, not the destination, that's what he kept telling me with the smile hanging in the sunshine. But if you jump off, there is even less of an answer, there isn't any answer in jumping off, even though it's all a big mistake, you have to stay with it and endure, isn't that right? That's right, he said. I didn't mind so much when that funny fellow loved my leg, then it wasn't so bad, even though it was only one leg. What's the difference? No difference. But when he went to sleep on the deck chair, well, it got bad again. If only he had stayed a little longer he might have made everything so much better, it's hard now, it's hard this way.

"Yes," he said, "I agree, he did help things for both of you."

"I watch him longingly out there so he doesn't know I'm watching him. I don't want to impose myself. I had my thing with him and now I have to stand behind this door and just remember, hope he'll find another leg, wish it still were one of mine. It was so nice, it's really hard to give it up, his attention, it's awfully hard to give all that up, the letters and the sonnets and incense, all of it, but it's an artistic accomplishment to discover how to be deserted, to fade out gorgeously, that's something too, like painting the great picture or writing the great novel, it's art, how to hide yourself away and not perish, and how to discover yourself and not perish, to have dignity to your wishing without feeling worthless."

"Yes," he said, "there's truth to what you say."

"All the same," I told him, "it hurts."

"I'm certain it must," he said.

Night was falling, a soft night, not the galloping black horse coming over the horizon with the black rider, whipping me with terror, some new kind of soft, light evening was coming in.

"I've painted a red band around my leg, near the top, it's to remind me that once there was a rich green time. That's all you can ask for, really, a time when it all was yours, and then the time is gone away, now it's another kind of time, a mellow time filled with remembering, not terrified. But the loving did make the difference. Now I watch him looking at the passing legs, I long for him, but it's not possible anymore. He'll always remember mine, that much is true. He wasn't much, I would have never noticed him if he didn't love my leg so much. Imagine, longing for someone you wouldn't have bothered with anyhow. But all the same, the intensity and the passion, and me being the one and only one, how he discovered me like that and made my leg this thing of value, that's what's so hard to lose. I mustn't think of it or I'll dissolve. He wasn't very interesting, really nothing much about him, dynamic he was not, not even unusual, just the intensity and the passion. It soared out of him like a fountain, and it made him come alive and take a place and become the one and only one and now I have to stand back here and watch, and wonder and remember. Do you understand what I'm telling you?"

"I do. I understand it all," the Smile said. "I understand it and I don't feel sorry for you, not one bit."

"You should," I said.

"Understanding is a very sad and lonely business," the Smile said to me, "but not pitiful.

"The Turtle's here, would you like him to come in?"

12

"Did you love him then?" he asked me. Yes, I think I did in that silent winter, but the film strip stopped, the moment of it all was caught and frozen there with the body hung in space, a slow-motion film strip when it stopped and all of it was held in slow motion—stopped. The picture never caught again, it just hung there like that, never quite reached him, never really touched, never could, the film was ended just like that before it began—always waiting for it to begin again but it never did.

The Turtle was massively large and always brinking on expansion. There he was, with black curly hair and black curly eyebrows and under them were little lines with eyes tucked deep inside. When he'd smile you couldn't see his eyes at all, no eyes, that's who he was, Smiling No Eyes. Everything was a joke to the Turtle, sad and terrible things made him laugh. Never mind, forget it, he would say, and laugh a little.

Something remote about him and making jokes all the same, remote and teasing and making tears, and then slipping away like smoke into another silence that was unbroken. I could never catch the Turtle, never put him in my hand, or a jar, or on a chair or sofa, he slipped away snickering and making jokes and gone. His silences were deep and complete. He lived in there somewhere, in a quiet, mysterious, No Trespassers kind of place. He came out only to be polite once in a while. When it was dreadful he would come out and help me. He would come out to hear his bedtime stories, the worse they were the better he liked it, and then he slipped away again, staring out the window, lighting a cigarette and not hearing, vanishing while sitting there, gone away with a blank look on his face and nothing to say.

Can I have a cigarette, I'd ask him. Sure, he'd say, and he'd give me one and he'd light it for me and smile. Then he'd look out the window again. There was nothing else to say.

I tried, I'm sure I tried. It wasn't hard to try, it was automatic, I just always try at first. I wore my nifty little sweatshirt that said HONEST FUCKING. Two trim nice and nifty little bosoms peeking out full of the rest of my life, just sitting there and waiting, but it all never happened, we skipped over the whole thing. We played ring-around-the-rosie around the whole thing we were all about and then we all fall down. That's how it was and is and always will be with the Turtle and me. I know because I don't care anymore. As long as I cared, it was different, I was different, but I stopped caring, and so there won't be anything else. There were smiles and tears and warm things but not many, not enough. It all got lost somehow, all caught up in the ring around my guts, the rope tightening around the place to breathe and fly, done. There was nothing really wrong with him, you've got to understand, I just couldn't reach, I don't know why, but I just couldn't reach. He never did mean things to me. He just wasn't, that's all, he just wasn't. Exactly like my brother said, and we played ring-around-the-rosie, forming only the border around everything real.

Oh how my brother made fun of him. My brother was bad to him at first, mean and bad, teasing him, pulling tricks and jokes on him, making a kind of fool of him whenever he could. I would watch my brother, I would hate to see the way he was, but I couldn't help feeling more and more separated from the Turtle all the same. I was ashamed of this, but it happened all the same. I drifted away more and more from the Turtle because my brother wasn't proud of him, wasn't impressed with him, you could tell that, that's what mattered, my brother wasn't impressed.

The Turtle never struck back, he vanished instead, he evaporated like mist, still smiling. I wished someone could overtake my brother, just once, just decently and fairly once in all my life stand up to him, and no one ever did. Maybe that's why I drifted away from the Turtle, maybe not. Maybe I always kept remembering, slow-footed, slow-thinking Turtle, can't you do better, better, better? Better is a painting hanging on a wall, playing the violin is better, what I could do better were things that didn't have to do with people, and still that wasn't good enough. My brother said not to give advice, that I didn't know what the world was really like. But better was how to write. I could really do that, couldn't I? Finally that was the only thing that better was for me. In that solitary struggle I could find my own self hiding and maybe save myself a little bit, but my brother took that too, even that he made me give to him and all that he gave me in its place was his vanity. Wait for me, he said, that was all he gave me in exchange.

The Turtle couldn't stand lies, he didn't understand them, not a bit. To him a lie was just that, something untrue, evil, or wrong. But lies aren't always, you know. Sometimes lies are art too, sometimes lies are creating, sometimes lies are wonderful, they can lift and soar and take you all away. I know this, I've lied like this telling people fantastic stories on trains and buses, cab drivers, strangers in hotel lobbies, wild lies that were short stories all in magical swiftness with dashes of color, with the wish and the secret and the poetry. "Life makes bad art," but lies are another kind of art, a quick art, a devastating art, when the lies are good, not just denials of truth. I would tell these lies and make people laugh and muse, but the Turtle would always say, Come on now, baby, that's just not so, and all of a sudden the moment was blank, the color was black, the room was dim and there was nothing to say, it couldn't be explained away, it was just over, all of it, the fun and magic and the secret between us, the language and the partnership were over. It's very difficult to make a secret understanding with another person who betrays you and betrays your nature, your essence, who betrays the dream you are sending off in firecrackers and smoke. But it's really all a dream, I mean, what you have to give someone and what they have to give back to you, it's really just the dream you need that they can help you with. It isn't the day-to-day living that makes the difference, it's the secrets and the illusions that you have about yourself and about him that you need to share and that you need to preserve and all the plans for a someday when the dream comes true. You have to swap fantastic stories about how great you are and how great he is and how good it's going to be, and not be made to feel ashamed for dreaming and daring to try to make your dreams come true. Somebody's got to help you, somebody's got to catch you if you fall, when you fall, and pick you up and brush you off and say, Look here, don't forget that dream, old girl, it's all you've got and you can't forget it, it doesn't matter what it is, it doesn't matter if it never happens, it's still the thing we share and you can't forget it.

But the Turtle couldn't do that with me. He took away the dream and gave me dead-end streets with things to be done and I dreamed a better dream than this. Old swanny girl. Come dance with me. Out upon the glass-top tables spin and twirl, great white swan who listened now and heard the heartbreak and was not indifferent. Are you happy in the fading pink of morning? Dance while I watch my fingers—dance. The sky was blue before, it wasn't always smoky gray flecked with seed pearls, teardrops beating on the window-panes. Dance before the sun goes down and write my little tiptoe story with your scratch marks in the sand, come dance with me.

And I came galloping in to the Turtle with apologies for things I didn't do, can you imagine? Breaking down before the mountain that was waiting there and waiting, tomorrow everything will be all right, it's always worse at night, but what's all right, what's worse? What gets better? Only dance, only dance with me and make the music come on louder, make it hurt my ears and keep on dancing with me, swanny girl, we love him, don't we, but he is gone away and there isn't much that can be done, isn't that correct?

The Turtle's here to see me, that's what you've said, in his great brown shiny shoes. How do you do? Badly all the same. I'm sorry. No you're not. Of course I am. Then if you were you would make it better somehow, you'd bring the swan to stay, you'd make something happen that would matter. If only you'd bring the swan to me, that much. I talk to her when I'm all alone. I talk to her.

But that's ridiculous.

That's what you always say, that's all you know how to say, why don't you try and do a thing that's full for me, just bring the swan to me, I long for her while I am here, just bring the swan.

How 'bout the priest?

How 'bout the swan?

If you believe on Jesus, all things are possible, he says, all things are real if you believe on Christ the savior, the great huge rambling wooden Turtle man. He held the Bible out to me.

I believe in swans, I tell him, I believe in white huge feather wings that catch the breeze and drift on silent summer streams, I believe in long white necks that bend, just to bend a little, this way and that, I believe in dancing clowns and blown-glass birds that have a nest of crystal feathers, I believe in pinks and greens and special purples splashed across a wall that sing a different kind of song. I want to come home, Turtle, I want to come back again and be real.

Does it run in families, the ability to finally stand alone at the top of the world? What's it like at the top of the world, does the wind hurt when it hits you in the face, can you look the wind in the face, Turtle? I'd like to marry someday and be sincere, I'd like to be faithful, full of monogamy and loyalty, I'd like to dedicate myself like the first page in a book, to someone, anyone, it doesn't matter who, it costs a lot of suffering to be free. I'd like to take another breath and try, not today, another day. I'd like the swan to come and be with me, I've depended on her for a long, long while, but it's always been only in my rememberings of her. I'm ready now to help her. A sense of worth is a solitary thing. I want to find my way again out of the glass forest. I'd like to paint my way back down the tan gray road to suppertime and being hungry. I want to survive and hope and make a vital commitment to myself, a commitment to just being alive and loving myself a little bit. Will you take me home with you?

The Smile is fading back beside the window, leaning and watching and listening. The Turtle is sitting on a chair with both feet on the ground. I'm standing in the middle of the room in a white hospital gown like a pillar that was once part of something more. I'm small and my toes are pointed in and my hands are folded down in front of me.

"I did a painting, Turtle man. A nice painting while I was here. Would you like to see it?"

The Turtle nods his head.

"I didn't show it to my brother when he came but it was for him, this girl I painted. I wanted him to love her. I wanted him to want her, to spend his life searching for her, to find her and keep her and make love to her like I once wanted you to touch her instead of me."

"Let's see the painting," the Turtle says.

There was the flying girl, soaring with rings on every finger, the juicy plumpness and the dreams all there. There it was and the freedom, the bounding airlight freedom done in wonderful shades of white and seed pearls, flowers blooming wide with suns and birds and stars and magic. There was the magic. There was the creation. There was the struggle liberated and there was the kind of truth that was universal like a smile is universal. Soaring freedom. The laughing flying girl broken free and soaring, up, up over the tops of buildings like a bird.

I did it at least on a piece of canvas and if only here at least I did it here. The painting was good, the Turtle said. He smiled and looked at it with his glasses on and then off and then on again, and yes, he thought it was really good. I liked that. He said he'd frame it. I liked that too. Writing might have meant more but I had to give that back to my brother. I didn't have the strength to fight for it. It takes a lot of giving up of childish things and a lot of strength to fight for something and I guess I never had that kind of strength. This was the shameful little fleeting bit of truth I peeked at while I flew across my calculations of myself and this was also what the painting meant, a compromise. Me connecting to a stretch of cloth and a spray of colors on a board. Me connecting to an ancient melody plucked out on a violin a long summer night ago. Shall I practice scales again or paint the girl I wished I could have been? I'll paint the girl. He wouldn't allow me any more. I understood.

I want to come home, I tell the Turtle. I don't want to hear the wailing anymore and I don't want to feel the dream. I've put them all in the seashell and have to keep them there, all of them. And maybe I can paint my way slowly and softly back into the center of another universe that's more peaceful, that whirls dreamless around all things real. Not to hear the music I can't dance to, not anymore. I want to forget.

Do you remember how I had to turn around and listen if I was coming in from somewhere rushing out of breath, I heard this low echoey thing wailing in that house. What was it, I would think. What was it with the screen door closing on summer nights, warm air hanging in so heavy, the wooden porch and my mother's clicking heels as she would walk across it to the door? Whatever it was, I don't want it. I am resolved.

"Where is he?" she would ask, her silk brocade shawl all around her skinny bony being in a nightgown. "Where is he, where did he go, did you see him?"

"No, I haven't seen him but he'll be back," I always told her. "He'll be back out there whistling in the evening, walking up the dusty road and whistling."

"Where were you?" I would ask him.

"Out," he said.

"She's looking for you, she's always looking for you."

"Tell her to suck," he said. "Tell her to suck and bite," and he kept on whistling.

"Who do you hate?" I would ask him.

"I don't hate anyone," he would say, biting into an apple, not looking. "I don't care enough to hate, just to get out of here one day and not come back again, it's a suck here, it's all a big suck."

But he did hate. I think about it now alone on summer nights that feel the way they used to, smell the way they used to. He must have hated to have done the things he did to me. How much he must have felt and hated and made me pay for all of it in the sun-filled room at the far end of the hall, down in the cellar, how much he must have felt and hated and cared and made me pay for all of it. Oh no, don't call it love, it wasn't, it was a lot of things but it wasn't love, don't fool me by telling me that, I won't believe you if you do. What was it then, you ask me, sitting there with both feet firmly on the floor and watching me. It was revenge for having been destroyed himself. His eyes are gray now, I noticed that when he was here to see me, his hair was kind of set in place, his clothes were high and reeking just a bit from being too well chosen, that kind of clothes with the jacket buttoned all the way up. I see him now, his head and body running down a country road struggling, with no one there to struggle with, arms flailing, wrestling, fending off a phantom, running, being chased with no one there behind him all the way, with the trees in rustic bloom all autumn red and orange all around him running running down a country road and coming, hunched up and coming all over a stop sign, clutching it and holding it and coming on it till he falls. My sister's face floods into my mind, looking through the window at the winter snow, I see her, her red hair and freckled face peering through the window at the driveway with the evening snow falling lightly, silently. I see myself in the little house behind the big city mansions with a boy whose name I never knew in that nameless timeless time when it was hot, and staying with him there and after him another one and then another one and then the beating of my heart in all the darkness and I clung to them and I wept. She was standing in the hall all that day, the sunlight flooded on the white stone floor, she was screaming at me—"She's dead and you're a whore, a dirty little tramp, what did I do to deserve this?" face all red and distorted like you would be seeing it through a ruby blown-glass vase. How strange and unreal she seemed to me. How far away the whole thing was when I stood there with the few things I could grab in a brown paper bag, only the brown paper bag was real. How watery and silent it's all become, standing there in that hall holding the bag and hearing it all silently around my eyes. I could almost see the three of us standing in front of our mother, holding hands in a circle, the red head thing of curls was smiling and laughing with the blond boy in the middle and me standing there, all holding hands in a circle going round and round as Mother stood in the middle, remote through the blocks of time, wrapped in her shawl in her own foggy cloud, through the days and nights, never leaving, never coming, never going away, always there, always humming to herself, never touching as we played in silence. It was all done in silence the way it was done to all of us. We tragic declarations of her weakness. We encumbrances to her endless daydreams, we meaningless realities; her songs that had no words. We were the things she looked past to filmy dancing shadows on the lawn, her summer days that had no beginning or no end. We were the possibilities she forsook that might have kept her real and flowing and pulsating, that might have made her laugh or cry or wait or narrow her eyes and listen, but it never happened like that for her in her brocaded shawls, remote, untangled, unentwined. In a monstrous way she wasn't even there, wasn't anything that we could recognize. Who was she then, standing there in the middle of our circle with her yellow lights staring out between the spaces that separated us? Who was she then, who was the portrait hanging over the fireplace in the dining room, the drafty old Victorian dining room reflecting better days—wearing black lace with an unlined face? Who was she? No one ever found that out. No one that we could ever smell or shake hands with even in a formal way and have to curtsy, even that would have been real. Who was she then, this person made of glass whose reflection echoed on the mirrored walls all around her? Just the wailing, that's who she must have been, the wailing empty lonely thing in all of us.

"Come on," the Turtle says, "we're going home."

PART III

13

Then take me disappearing through the smoke rings of my mind,
down the foggy ruins of time,
far past the frozen leaves, the haunted frightened trees,
out to the windy beach, far from the twisted reach
of crazy sorrow.
Yes, to dance beneath her diamond sky with one hand waving free,
silhouetted by the sea, circled by the circus sands, with all
memory and fate driven deep beneath the waves.
Let me forget about today until tomorrow——

Bob Dylan

"Where are you going, Turtle?" I ask him.

"Away," he says, "but I'll be back."

"Why are you leaving?" He's putting his things in the old tattered suitcase that once belonged to his mother, his shiny new shoes and toothbrush, his gum massager and aspirin, his new pajamas and underwear. "Why are you going, Turtle, big old daddy Turtle man, why are you going away?" I'm not smiling now while he puts his belongings into the suitcase silently, his shirt is open at the neck, his tie is loose, his stomach is bulging over his belt, the great old Turtle is getting fat and more flat-footed, his looks got sloppy, he looks bad in the summertime with something oily about him and falling apart in a contained sort of way. He looks much older. It looks like it hurts him, something, and I'm watching the thing that looks like it hurts.

"It's all my fault, isn't it, Turtle, about you going?" I ask him. "Tell me it's all my fault, and tell me I did it to you, I never meant to, Turtle."

"Not to worry," he answers me, "just not to worry."

It's almost a year since the little girl died—he has stayed—can't leave yet.

Dear Turtle [I will write him],

Don't go away, stay, it wasn't your fault about the car, it wasn't all your fault. I'm sorry about the things I said that day, I'm really sorry about how people beat each other into nothing and wonder why and say they love each other.

It was an accident. It was just an accident. I need you, Turtle, somewhere out there wherever you are going, I really need you. The child is dead, our little girl is dead and how you cried in the hall next to her body in the hospital. I couldn't cry [I'll tell him], at first I couldn't cry but I heard you when they wheeled me away, I heard you crying. I still hear you crying, don't go away. But still I haven't cried. I didn't do my best, I held the wheel of the car, that's all I did, and let her die, do you hear me, Turtle, I let her die, not you, and though you said I did my best, I didn't. Only I know that, only I can swear to that. Don't go away, I wished my best, I prayed my best, but I didn't do anything, I didn't do a fucking thing but let her die, I was angry at you when I left the house, I was so angry at you when I got into the car and started going to buy, what was it, oranges, a dozen oranges, that's right, and some liverwurst for lunch, and I was raging mad at you for sleeping there, not even getting up to say a word to me that whole day, I drove crazy, Turtle, but it was still an accident. It will be a year on Tuesday. I need you, don't go away, come back, stay.

I'm watching him, he's standing there on the movable steps, the great silver bird is waiting like a giant penis ready to take wing and own the skies. He's waving. He's looking lost out there, waving to me with his briefcase in his hand,

128

and I'm waving back to him, the tears streaming down my cheek.

"I'll completely change," I shout to him, "when you come back I'll have completely changed."

"Not to worry," he says again, and there are tears I see him wipe away.

The August sun is glazing everything in a white heat, finding a car out there in a field of cars, rows of cars, sections of cars all with the scorching August sun beating down on them and baking them and roasting them and diminishing them to melting steel. The roads wind in and out and over and under each other. Driving through the massive interplay of highways with cars coming at me and passing me, over me, and circling under me in the straight ahead for an endless nothing stretch of bad feelings. I feel bad. The Turtle's gone away.

The Turtle hated change, I craved it, action, motion, restless changing things around, but he couldn't stand a chair moved out of its spot. I moved the chairs around for the sheer joy of changing things, he was afraid of change. I threw things out, he would stand under the window and catch the falling debris and put it back on the shelves again. I couldn't stand accumulation, old things, useless belongings. I gave them away as fast as they accumulated, tossed them on the world that had its hands stretched out for them, and I smiled, laughed, but he expected one day to find a million uses for a billion useless things. I was restless, he was slow. I got lost in the involvement, he restricted where he went, where his feelings could lead him. I had no reservations, he had tiny plans, I stood people up, never returned phone calls, flung his shoes out of the portholes of the ship, left people waiting for me in hotel lobbies, never showed, didn't give a shit. He used to perspire, mop his head at first until he got to doing it too and laughing about how lousy it was, the things we were doing, laughing a nervous static belching laugh, but he got a lot like me and liked it, and that was something, wasn't it? He got a lot like me and it made him scared, but he still changed, didn't he? Even though he tried to hold things down, he slowly changed, and that meant something, didn't it?

Dear Turtle,

It's hot, it's so awfully hot, there's nowhere to put myself, it's so hot these days, where are you? I begged you for another car, I told you the one I had had something wrong, I couldn't manage it, not from the very beginning. I'm sorry to bring it up again but I begged you for another car, why wouldn't you hear me, why wouldn't you listen? Did you think I was crazy? Did you think I didn't know what I was talking about? The city's hot, there is a blanket on everything, a dulling oppression. I've managed fairly well in spite of it. I've been able to manage but when I think about her, I stop. Forget it, I say, you've got to forget it or you'll die again and again, you've got to be strong, and I try, I really do, but it's so hard, old Turtle, it's so hard. You stayed with me at first out there beside the trees, you stayed with me and said I did my best, smoking hash and seeing her everywhere we looked, but you stayed with me and now you've gone, it's bad again now that you're gone. It will be a year on Tuesday, like I told you, I know you don't care about anniversaries, things like that, you say they don't exist, but it's hard all the same, the time of year and seasons and remembering make it hard again. About the car, there was something there I couldn't do a thing with. It seemed to go all by itself. You would have listened to me if you thought I really couldn't manage it, if you had believed me, then you would have listened, but you never took me seriously, never. You've always given me things I couldn't use, why? Is it because you've never heard me?

Two huge fighting mating dogs came out from the side of the road, I slammed on brakes that weren't there, isn't that right, Turtle, and I went into the tree and she was killed all across the windshield of a car you wouldn't hear a word about. Whose fault, no one's, just the deafness all over again, just the blindness and the not hearing. I loved that child, Turtle, I loved her terribly much, my little girl with the golden ringlets, and the song she always sang, I really loved

130

her enough, or else I'd be dead now too, I couldn't have survived that accident if I didn't love her as much as I did, but I'll never get over it, will I, I'll always be hanging on like this, won't I? Never mind, I say, it's no one's fault, whose fault, I drove the car, my fault, you know, I guess, but what's the difference? Can we say it's the dog's fault? Yes, that's good enough, the mating fighting dogs, they killed my child. I don't want to hate you, I want to live—I hurt too bad to hate or blame or see or hear another thing but healing all over again. Are you coming back on Tuesday, will you let me know, it's hot here, I don't know what to do with myself, the heat's so bad. Where are you, Turtle, somewhere up there in that giant silver flying penis that owns the sky and judging me.

You shouldn't have gone, you know, you shouldn't have turned away from me like this, it's hot here in the city, it's so hot, Turtle, I don't do so well all alone. I need.

No letters came, no calls, not a word. Was there ever really a Turtle after all, was there somewhere in the world a man called Turtle who had shared that child with me?

And Tuesday came alone and hot, a morning coming up out of the night, starting out in purple heat and spreading like a hand.

"I have to stay alive," I told him, I told this splendid brand-new man who suddenly made me understand I had to stay alive. I met him the first time in the park when I took the boy to feed the ducks, when I clung to the boy after the Turtle went away, there he was, this golden man. He was tall with yellow hair straight and falling over his ears, over his collar, he was very tall, very big with a navy blue sweater and an old shaggy tweed jacket with marvelous corduroy trousers and great, huge, fine and delicate hands. I saw his hands almost before I saw his face, these great beautiful hands that understood. His hands were gentle. But the way he walked was bold, as though he had a shaft of arrows on his back and wings on his shoes, as though he carried a bow made of gold, and every now and then he might get up from the park bench he was sitting on and strut out across the little patch of grass and take an arrow from the case and put it to the bow and shoot it, high, very high, and it would sail, as if by such enormous skill or magic, to the sun. He was the golden archer man.

"A very bad thing has happened to me, I lost a child. I lost a little girl in a car accident, I drove the car," I told him. We were alone now in the springhouse in the dark.

"These two huge, fighting mating dogs ran out and I slammed on brakes that weren't there. I went into this giant oak tree. Oak trees kill, love kills, deafness kills, blindness kills, abandoning kills, turning away from someone when they need you kills, dogs kill, all over, everywhere you look there are huge essential dangers, and it's very easy to get killed."

He was listening in the dark with a yellow blanket around his shoulders and this new, almost strange and almost familiar face began to cry.

"Don't cry," I told him, "it's not for you to cry, just to understand that the killing isn't going to stop as long as the blindness is still there, all the blindness, the deafness. The Turtle is my husband, he never understood a word I said. That killed our child. No, don't say a word in his defense, it isn't necessary. I myself have forgiven him because I understand, but in understanding it still doesn't change a thing, not for the child who is dead, not for me who had to keep on living in the dark, hearing my own words echo back to me without answers. He went away, I don't know where he went, away was all he said to me. I have an address on a little slip of paper, and I sent the letters there, but they are never answered. He said he'd be back and I believe he will, but it's not important, either way, it doesn't matter."

"How old are you?" he asked me. "Thirty-three," I told him. The little room, the little springhouse at my mother's

house, dark, tired, old, so old by now and everything was falling away and decaying.

"Was this where you grew up, here?" he asked me. "Yes,"
I told him, "I've always lived here all my whole life, no matter where I've lived it's always been here. I had a sister but
she died, my brother moved away long ago, my mother and
the swan are all that's left, my father, he was never here at
best, and when he died the place began to fall apart, the
house, the gardens, all of it, just falling apart. She'll have to
sell it soon, I guess, or die, either way, there won't be many
more summers. But I like it here, I like to come and bring
the boy, he likes it here. You should have seen it years ago, it
was marvelous, this great Victorian matriarch pitched across
the grass, in her time. She's an old decrepit lady finally. Her
jaws are sunken in, her face is lined and ravaged, her body
slipped away to chipping paint and broken pipes, it's sad.
When my father was alive he kept the place in stoic perfec-
tion, he never let a blade of grass be out of step, there were
no odors except mustiness or cleaning agents. He was an
hourglass that trickled one grain at a time, in perfect tune,
he trickled all the time, he never never lost a minute, he was
never out of step."

He was watching me, listening, watching as if his breath
was coming from his eyes, his eyes were eating me.

"Do you think I'm pretty?" I asked him.

"Yes," he said.

The semidarkness began to smell of flesh and something
oily, his hands reaching for me couldn't wait, breathing fast
and greedy for me, purging my mind for just a while in all
the semidark with light coming in from the windows with
the cobwebs, the spider coming down her rope of silk to investigate who has come again, who is here, the newsy gossipy
little spider comes to get a look and hurries back again to
where it is safe. There is something stronger than pain, something better than whiskey to make you forget. A man who
wants you, who really wants just and only you in all the dark,

life, a way back, the way, the road, the direction, the rebirth.

The springhouse in the dark, no lights, musty from no fresh air or tending, dust and cobwebs hanging in, the air heavy in the dark with this new man again.

Slow-motion figures gliding in silence without words to one another, a man and a woman, arms out, feet lightly touching the ground, two bodies fluid, floating, reaching, nearing, touching one another lightly in silence, in slow motion, and the camera didn't stop, this time the camera didn't stop, it wasn't frozen on the silent screen this time forever. A man and a woman without a tinge of impurity, without realization of a world around them, without a thought. In the dark he touched my face with his fingers, in the silent dark I touched his hair and lips, no words, just the finding in the dark. "Is it real?" I asked him. "Yes," he shook his head, "it's real."

Into the place where finding stopped and need was starting, a need diluted by a sense of joy and happiness, into the night with the smell of it coming from his mouth and skin and limbs. The smell of the body—the smell of a man and a woman together in the oily dark, the heavy, dry and oily dark. And a man and a woman finding in that dark all the many things that one another are. The smell of a man and woman fucking.

"Will you tell all of this to your mistress?" I asked him after, "will you tell her all about it?" And he starts to laugh. His laughing fills the room, bellowing, hard, uproarious laughing. He pulls himself up and throws back his head and is laughing. I watch him, very happy. There was something honest moving between us, something truthful and free, something completely without hesitation or shame, something pure. That's what freedom is, something between two people that is truth. . . . And I can almost see the little wooden soldiers lined up by the wall, the light falling across the floor in blocks, the trees outside. The window never changes, only the generation of leaves that come and go.

Where are they? she would call. Where are the children? It's almost dinnertime.

We're out here, he would holler back, we'll be right in.

The blankets that we brought have made the bed with a yellow blanket around his shoulders. It's cool tonight, August nights are always cool.

"Would you do a favor for me, a silly little favor?"

"Yes," he said.

"Would you lie on top of me and put your hand across my mouth to silence me, just for a moment, and if I close my eyes almost all the way, your yellow hair is all that I can see, just for a moment, will you?"

"Once there was a child," he began, "my child, a little girl like yours. She went to play one day and never came back, we found her body in the woods behind the house, strangled dead, the boy next door." He was sitting straight on the floor staring straight ahead of him, not seeing anything but that day when he found the child and the days that followed, the nights and the days till it found a spot in him and nestled down there to squat forever.

As he told me the story, my mind went back to a newspaper headline ripping through me of the child, of the day, and I remembered all of it. It happens many times, I've read about such things before and after that particular child, but I remembered her for all these years, somehow strangely I remembered her, I never knew who the child was, I never knew the parents, but I remembered all of it and the way the father wrote a letter that the paper published, begging for forgiveness for the boy, begging for help for him, for help for all the millions like him that might have done the same but didn't, just by something lucky, the other hemmed-in, suffering, sick, and lonely other boys who didn't. And here was the father now telling it to me, what I remembered in some vague and far-off way, the little girl who had stayed with me vaguely for all the years since then. Did I in some strange way know that this was him? Did he in some less strange way remember my own headlines of the accident? Was this part of our drawing to each other? Reaching out to try and bear it better, not quite so all alone with another who could understand. Was this the alliance?

"I love to sing," he said, "do you know? Anyhow I love to sing even though something has gone all rotten with the world."

His yellow hair fell straight across his eyes, his blue eyes and his long thin body.

"I love to sing," he said.

Walking in the woods fast, holding hands together and laughing, stopping by the creek and watching the fisherman out there and laughing. Going to the beach and lying in the sand, feeling the hot sand on our feet, feeling us baking into the sand, becoming sand and dissolving near the sea. "I have a brother," I began, "you'd like him, he looks a lot like you, or at least he did."

"Yes," he says, "you've mentioned him before."

"Anyway," I say, "would you come with me one day and meet him, would you like that?"

"Maybe," he says, "maybe one day."

I am real again waiting for the phone to ring, staring at the phone and waiting. Waiting for the rose to open in slow motion, waiting for the rain to stop, waiting for the day to start, waiting for the night to pass into another day of waiting. Gratitude is the purest form of love, love is a lot of things. Gratitude is part of it, one part. I became the rose that was opening in slow motion. I became the flowing gratitude that touched kindness and light on everything I passed. I became the wood song, dancing in the rain with my hair cut short and my body grown slim and long and loose, with the palms of my hands turned out, my fingers spread wide. Failure and fantasy were a little ball I threw to the sun. I was free of yesterday and tomorrow and once upon a time, all at once, I was free of all of it. Where once the slow-motion movie stopped with the two people caught forever in a time-less freeze, hair blowing in the wind, arms stretched out in smiling lightness dancing in slow motion. It started again from there with him now where the Turtle used to be and the figures met and touched and were real again, all real and living color, real.

"I want a baby," I began, "I want a baby child with you," and he was silent and he stared at me. Life was flooding back without the thing of gravity or weight, a weightless, light, and aboveground love with nothing snagged. Reunions in the springhouse. The swan was old and watched it with a heavy heart, I could tell she had a heavy heart. It's all illu-sion, she would say to me. Don't be fooled, it's illusion. It's the dream, she said, it's just the dream, and she heaved a sigh and went on back to sit beneath the trees.

Oh no it's not, I told her, swanny girl, this time I've found it all, this time it's real and I can have it, I have to have it, this time it's not a dream. I'm not going to paint for a long, long time, I choose life.

You'll find out, she said, one day you'll find out. You bet-ter stick to painting, you better go in the places where you can, the swanny sighed.

Cobwebs in the windows of the springhouse, the spider spinning on and not a hint of scandal there, just industry. The dust was thick, so thick we wrote our names in it.

"I want a child," I began, "a baby, the little girl we both have lost." He looked at me and didn't answer.

He came and went like the summer rains. He appeared and was gone without a word, only to return again and stay and in the in-between I drifted, light without gravity. I waited like the rose opening in slow motion and he returned. Nights were little chunks of eternity, the rains were thick that year, full rich crops of rain, dancing on the roof and licking and spattering against the windowpane. They came like little magic people to circle us in the nights and insulate us and separate us from all the rest of time, they were our rains, our summer band of magic merry music. They belonged to us.

"Watch it," the swan would say, "it's not what you think."

And I laughed at her. "You're getting old, you've forgotten all of it. It's real, I tell you." While I touched his face in wordless finding I knew it all was real. "Is it real?" I asked him, and he said "Yes," he said it all was real. "See the way the sun falls on certain parts of the trees creating dimension and depths? All real."

The swan said that the only thing real is change. She cocked her head and looked at me.

Who's taking care of your child while you dream? she asked me.

Let me tell you about him, Madam Swan, I said. I always tell you things. I always tell you everything, although so often it doesn't make a bit of difference to you anyhow. Most of the time you keep a steady little murmur going on that's all your own, no matter what's crashing around you. You never lose your beat. I ought to listen to you but I never do. I just hear you and run away cursing what I hear. *But this time, swan, you're wrong.* He and I are alike, he and I are the same people, two from that great army of abandoned children who have found each other, ah yes, that's who we are.

You're not children anymore, or didn't you know that? she yawns.

Never mind.

His father dived into a little lake that he had dived into a million times before, strange about it, he dived so many times in this lake so he should have known where the rocks were, where it was shallow. The golden archer man is an expert diver. You should see the way he dives and leaps into the water and swims the mile up and back without looking out of breath, he has enormous strength, but his father died on the rocks. His father broke his neck where he should have known that it was shallow water. His mother left him then with his grandmother, this old ancient woman in a big house without other children, without other people, just servants. There was one servant girl who was good to the little archer man, she took him in her bed at night and sang to him and showed her body to him, showed him her breasts that stood up like little mountains. He said they looked like little mountains to him and he touched them and she touched him in the dark and he explored her and she explored him and no one ever knew. But she went away one day, the grandmother sent her away. She was crying when she left and he was aching for her and when he asked his grandmother, the old lady told him that the servant girl was wicked and evil, that she was a bad person and that's why she was sent away. The archer man was all alone after that and empty. He searched for her through the streets of the small town where he lived, he searched for her everywhere. There was a great iron fence around the school where he was sent and he would stand hanging on the fence through all his lunchtimes and recess times looking for her to come for him as she always had come for him. He sat in class looking out the window that looked on the great iron fence but she didn't come again, she never came. It took him a long time to believe she wasn't coming back, like his mother wasn't coming back, and when he finally did, he began to study. He turned to books with all the feelings that he once had given her. He became a brilliant student, he took every honor, every prize. His grandmother was proud of him but he hated his grandmother and with all the hate he felt for her he turned even more to his studies. As soon as he could, he left his grandmother's house. He left without too many dreams, he took all his books and went but he was always searching for the servant girl. He said he was always hungry and thirsty, no matter how much he had, still he always went begging because he was so hungry and thirsty all the time. I understand this, Madam Swan, you can't imagine how good it feels to understand.

Now he's a great archer who sends his arrows to the sun, alone, a fire sign, mercurial, he shifts in his own silences and moods.

I showed him the porch of my mother's house, the screen door, I led him through from the attic to the cellar, I showed him the stained-glass window that didn't look out, the play rooms, and the study lined with books that no one ever looked at anymore. I showed it all to him and tried to tell him what it once was like, the yellow daffodils in spring, the sunlight flooding the hallway, the organdy curtains, the milk chocolate evenings coming on sweet and rich.

My mother was in a chair beside the window, old, withered, alone. Her nurse was writing at the table in the corner. My mother had taken to religion in purple velvet dressing gowns with seven, ten, maybe fifteen bands of rosaries around her neck, maybe fifteen little crosses with a Jesus hanging down around the place a bosom might have been. "Ah yes," she says, "we don't have many guests here anymore, we try to keep it very private, we don't like the public milling around, no more of that riffraff. Would you like to see the paintings? Take the gentleman to see the paintings," she tells an invisible being near her arm, and we're respectful. We leave and return to the springhouse and tell each other about it all, and pick it apart and put it together again and make love.

He understood the impossibility of reality. He could draw a little circle around madness and point it out and hold it in his hand without losing his own sanity, without becoming it. He didn't laugh at it, he didn't run from it, he understood.

"Poor woman," he says, "poor tragic woman all locked up inside herself. She only combed her own hair all her life. Monkeys groom each other, they pick the lice and nits from

140

each other's heads, they study little spots and scrutinize the other with total commitment, scratching at each other and digging with their nails, examining and dedicated. It's good, it's good that way. It's love."

"I want a baby," I told the archer man. "The great Gingerbread Fortress is crumbling, there won't be many summers anymore, I want a baby. The Turtle will be coming back one day, the swan will die, there aren't plans that I can make except to have a baby, your baby. That's the only thing that's real, the only thing that's enough all by itself, the only thing that doesn't break your heart, that doesn't leave you, that doesn't change, a baby."

He used to bring bourbon to the springhouse and I used to bring chocolate, bags of little silver chocolate kisses, chocolate cookies, chocolate cake, and I ate the chocolate while he drank the bourbon and we used to have a feast. It was marvelous, swan, you should have come instead of floating out there prophesying and looking leery and skeptical. You should have joined us instead of always warning and whispering under your breath. It would have made you so happy because we were children again running up the hill, it was almost as though it was my brother's blond hair flying, his face flushed and happy, just like his long thin body moving weightless, almost in slow motion. It was so like a dream, you can't imagine, running up the hill with the golden archer man, that for a moment I was the child again, I was young and pretty with no shoes, airlight, and he was even wearing a blue shirt and dungarees. You would have felt young again too, you would have smelled the spring.

He's back, he's here, Mother, he came back, look, come see, he came back. Watch the way the sun streaks across his face, it's him, come look. Go tell Mother he is back, she will want to know, she will be able to come and see him for herself. We're children, Mother, and you're not old and crazy, sitting locked up all inside yourself.

Look, he's laughing, running lightweight up the hill.

"I'm back," he shouts, "I'm back," but there was no sound, old swan, the picture was exact but there was no sound.

Ridiculous you say, you stupid swan, what do you know? What do you know of poetry and illusion, what do you know about the dream? All you understand are crusts of bread and a nap these days, you don't know another thing. You can't feel it anymore inside you, beating, beating, life and color and bursting out in spring when all the world was yellow lace. The red-head girl? You mustn't ask about her, it doesn't help a thing, she's gone, that's all, gone and done, why do you have to bring things up that should be left alone. She's gone away and anyhow, she never liked you, did you know. I'm frightened, I'm scared and frightened. Have you got a cigarette, old swanny girl?

My little girl is gone away with her, do you have a drink, old swan, a little swig of something strong and burning going all the way down? I like the way it burns its way to nothing and then I'm airlight and don't mind all this remembering.

I asked the golden archer man to dance with me out on the grass but he refused. He told me to be more serious. He told me to reflect and not to smile so much. He told me I was going wrong out there on the grass, that I was chasing something that wasn't there, can you imagine? He told me I was playing games and wearing costumes and though it was somewhat enchanting, it wasn't enough to hold onto for the rest of his life, me chasing shadows on the lawn. That's when I left for the beach. I took the boy and went to the beach. I was confused, I was frightened. He wanted me to marry him he said, he said he could love the boy and he would take care of us but I'd have to be more serious, I'd have to stop chasing phantoms on the grass, something like that. That I'd have to be more industrious, take a job, stop smiling so much. I asked him if he loved me and he couldn't answer, not a fast yes, or a smile, or a pull and a kiss, nothing like that, his face contorted and he looked like he was in pain and he started to sing, every time I asked him if he loved me he would sing. But yes, he wanted to marry me. That's when I went to the beach. He wanted me to leave the Turtle. How many times it occurred to me to leave the Turtle, but when it came like that, I ran away.

I'm eating a lot of chocolate, swanny. That's all I eat these days, chocolate days, candy breakfasts with a Coke, a chocolate milkshake for lunch with seven chocolate cookies, chocolate roast beef for dinner with a chocolate sweet potato, and never a pimple, never an extra pound. Would fall apart without it, keeps me alive, it matters. And oh, my God, my goodness, chocolate pudding. I scan the world for the richest, thickest, darkest chocolate I can find, I smell it and lick it and hold it in my hand and when it gets all soft and slippery, I suck it up and feel it coat the inside of my mouth with sweet softness sliding down and gone. My chocolate days and nights, they're good, old lady swan, maybe not the best way that there is, but I do it all with chocolate all the same.

The golden archer man looked so like my brother, didn't he? Even the way his bones were around his eyes when the light fell on him in the evening. My brother would have liked him, really liked him, my brother would have been impressed, I think. I kept thinking that when we were together, My brother would really like you, he'd be impressed with you, I'd show him how I could have a splendid man like you, and that would really fix my brother good . . . (and then what?)—then my mind went blank. I stared off into space and my mind went blank, that was the end of the road. There was nothing more to think. I saw the way my brother would see him, how my brother would respond and that he was mine, that he belonged to me, that he was the answer I had to all the clippings my brother's secretary sent to me, that he was what I gave up writing for, he was my prize, something that my brother would have really liked, and my brother couldn't have him, only me—so my mind went blank, there was nothing more to think. He wasn't the Turtle, and if he wasn't the Turtle, my brother might take him away from me like he took everything away from me. I was safe with the Turtle, nobody would want him, nobody would take him away from me.

The golden archer man could tell me about the universe, and the way the galaxies were formed, he could recite poetry in four different languages. I walked with him and heard him identify every manner of growing thing out there, every bird and every different compound of the earth, but when I asked him if he was happy walking out there with me he got silent and withdrawn and unreachable, then something was over that took a long time to get back to and try with once again. If I reached out to touch his hand he let me touch it but he didn't close in on mine in response, he simply went on talking and his hand, that most beautiful gentle hand, didn't answer. That's when I went to the beach, when his hand didn't close in on my own. I put the child in the car and drove all that day until it was night and from all sides was coming the low flat green land with water and sailboats and the sky which seemed to take up all the space there was.

You can't imagine, swan, what went on down there, at the party. I put the boy to sleep and got dressed in a room the hostess gave us.

"Where's the Turtle?"

"He's gone," I told her, "but he'll be back, he's coming back, he had to go away."

The house was set right on the beach, twenty steps away was sand and beyond that the black ocean with no moon, no stars, just the black ocean that went out to the sky and the white waves breaking near the beach. There were enormous hordes of people in wild fancy clothes, sunburnt and slim and streamlined, lying in hammocks on the porch, reclining in sun chairs, all their faces were stony deadpan straight with bright yellow lights. The music was all you heard coming from a speaker box, no one talked, they just stared ahead of themselves at nothing, they passed the joints around and everybody took a drag. I did too, but it didn't turn me on. Over in the corner three younger men tripped out on acid, laughing, roaring with laughter, talking about cosmic forces urging them to laugh, to understand, to see the meaning of the universe. I took another drag of grass, I held it deep inside me and I watched, nobody was moving, nobody was talking except the three younger men in the corner at a card table laughing about the meaning of the universe. I went over to them and sat down.

"What's your meaning?" the first one said.

"I haven't found that out yet," I answered them. "I don't know exactly, I only know what isn't my meaning," and they all began to laugh again at that.

"Would you like to drop a tab," the first one said, "and then we can find out what it is you're all about?"

"Sure." I didn't care, it didn't matter. The great golden archer man would be calling me by now, my phone would be ringing and he would be wondering where I was. He wouldn't be able to find me, and soon, in a day or two, he would stop trying. The Turtle was somewhere. Who knew where he was? It was weeks since he went away, weeks since I heard a word.

"Yes, I'd drop a tab."

At first nothing happened. Still the silent, beautiful, well-groomed, long-lined, streamlined people lying in reclining chairs and hammocks without expressions. At first it was still the music coming from the speaker box on the wooden porch and the beach and the ocean and the sound of the waves breaking on the beach in perfect time. But slowly it began to work, this little colored thing I took. Slowly my head began to feel heavy and thick, a kind of dizzy feeling, and the climb, rushes and more rushes of sensation through my body, like coming and coming without orgasm, pounding heart and feeling the blood flushing to my face, feeling the breath pushing out of me, feeling the tingling almost panicky feeling over all of me, the jumpy throbbing rushed excitement all over me to the top, and I looked around and all of it was slowly changing in slow motion. The walls of the house, the wooden castle walls began to breathe, bulging in and out with life, the door that was opening seemed to fly at me bigger than life, and I jumped back afraid it would hit me. I began to laugh, how funny, how enormous, the glass door blowing at me like a wind had swept it off its hinges. The people in the hammocks were made of water now, dripping over the sides of the hammocks, they were dripping into puddles on the wooden porch, puddles of themselves, and I ran to scoop them up and hand them back to themselves.

"But I'm pure," I told them all, "you see I'm really pure," and my three friends beside me began to laugh.

"It's the cosmos that we have to investigate, do you understand, the cosmos? What have you found out about it all?"

One of the men, it must have been a man, turned into a great green enormous turtle, the largest turtle that I ever saw, the most brilliant green, and there was a rope around him.

"Look! My husband, my turtle husband over there sleeping on the floor, I have to pick him up." I moved in a kind of airless way to where this great green sleeping thing was lying on the porch but when I got there he turned into a bag of Christmas tree balls and I stepped on him and I crushed him and I heard the tinkling glass and I began to laugh with my three friends who came to investigate with me.

"He wasn't my husband after all. He was the spirit of Christmas," and we laughed some more.

The waves looked like great mouths of wild animals screaming out at me and I turned, I didn't want to see that, the patterns on the walls began to move, and I turned. I didn't want to see that either. The floor began to breathe in and out and I looked up, I didn't want to see that.

146

"It's a bummer," I began to scream, "it's going to be a bummer and I'm scared."

"It's the cosmos, you've just forgotten." My friend held me by the arm. "Think about the cosmos, tell me what you see, don't panic, think about the cosmos, tell me what you find."

"I'm a crumb on the floor, I fell from a piece of bread, they are going to sweep me into the carpet sweeper in the morning. I'm so tiny and so unimportant that nothing matters. I'm incredibly insignificant. I'm an ant, a flea, and my lifetime of sixty years or more are sips of water in an ocean of tears."

"Yes," they said, "that's right, tell us more, tell us more about exactly how small you are."

"I never mattered anyhow. Life is original, death is ordinary. I am saved by my own insignificance. I see my face at fifty-three years old. I'm old and wrinkled. I have snow-white hair done up in a knot behind my head. I'm knitting in front of a fireplace with my brother, he is sitting there with me. He is old too, his face is ashen white and his hair is gray. He is eating an apple and belching. Our lives are insignificant. We have done nothing and we will continue to do nothing but wait for death. We never lived, my brother or I. I see my father and mother dancing on a wooden porch beside the sea. They are laughing, holding each other tight. They are young, almost children, happy and full of music. My brother and I are watching them, old and weary and white and lifeless.

"What's happened to the world? Something's gone all rotten."

I see the archer man in the woods with the body of his child, strangled, hanging from the branches of a tree, my brother is crying beside the tree, his tears become a puddle of blood and my little girl is drowning in the puddle.

"It's a bad trip," I scream. My heart is pounding out of me. I can feel my heart about to explode. "Save me from it, save me from it, please." I start to run from the porch to the beach, heading for the monster waves that are shouting, "Over here, come on, come here," as they opened and closed their ugly white enormous mouths. "Come on, I'm waiting for you, over here."

I was running on the beach for what seemed like hours with someone chasing me, hollering after me to wait for him, to stop running, to hold on and wait for him, but I kept on running. It was a starless night, the fog and mist hung in low and all along the other side the houses seemed to be like faces laughing at me, blinking their eyes, grinning, roaring, throwing back their heads and howling in gales of laughter. And still the waves were breaking their enormous white mouths and I kept on running up the beach, trying not to look to either side until he caught me.

At first he looked like my brother but I couldn't tell.

"Are you my brother, are you really him?"

I peered at the person standing there, narrowed my eyes and peered at him.

"No," he said, "I'm not your brother."

"Then who are you?"

"What's it matter who I am," he said, "you won't remember tomorrow."

"A bad trip," I told him, "a really bad one."

I saw my whole life, I saw everything I've ever tried to forget, it all came over me in color. I saw my old age. I saw my father and mother fucking. I saw them making me, my father was drunk and threw her down on the bed laughing and she screamed, "No, I don't want another baby, please no, not tonight, don't ruin everything." My father pulled off her clothes and tried to make sweet love to her but she fought him so he fucked her mean, nasty, huffing and panting and brutal and wet all over her and she screamed like it hurt her and then I saw this wiggling snake crack open this huge whitish yellow egg, and it spun around and around and around and then it started to scream too and shout and wail, "I AM."

It was a grotesque me. It had black oily straight hair and

my face with the body of a toad swimming around in water wailing, "I AM."

That wasn't all I saw. I saw all the creatures of the earth like tiny microscopic bugs wriggling on their backs, helpless, small, and scared. I saw evil forces needing to destroy, great winds of evil sweeping over the bugs wriggling there, great black winds that wiped out purity, creativity, innocence, and decency, big black monster clouds that sucked up the good from the earth and left only skeleton shells where life had been. Destruction, the need in man to kill, I saw it everywhere, on everything, endangering everyone, this endless horrible spirit of disaster settling on humanity like a fog. There was a feeling through all of it of hopelessness, of death, and there was no way out, no possibility anymore, the whole thing had gone too far, past the point of change, the course was set for all the rest of time. This was the way the world was.

The night was warm. I stood with him with our feet in the water, my heart still pounding almost out of my chest, his arms around me, his face pressing against my own and he held me and he shook his head to say, yes, he understood.

"Who are you?" I asked him. "Will you tell me who you are?"

"I'm the spirit of Christmas you crushed with your foot and heard the breaking glass. I was the green thing in the corner you came to look at and I watched you and I kept on watching you, half hoping this would happen so I could rescue you. A lot of people have tried to rescue you, I guess, but no one has, isn't that true?"

"Wait," I told him. That's not all I saw. I saw a court with a judge who was a penguin with a man's face, there was a golden jury box off to the left with other penguins with human faces and when they heard the truth spoken they put their arms around one another and began to cry, to weep with trembling happiness at the sound of truth, and when lies were said, when there was real injustice, they turned purple and froze on the spot and immediately there was the kind of morality one expected when he was four or five years old, something right or wrong and recognizable instantly, the way you thought it was when you were little, the clear-cut perfect sort of decency you were led to believe existed. I was brought on trial for the death of my child, killed in an automobile accident. They sang to me from the jury box with outstretched arms, they sang to me a marvelous song and the judge jumped down and danced with me a mad ferocious dance, throwing me out and pulling me in with fancy steps and dips and twirls, like a party, and I began to sing with them eventually. It was all merry and marvelous. I don't understand why it was so, something in a way to show they understood in the highest way, which a celebration usually is. That was good. I liked that part, it made me understand a lot of things about the inadequacies of intention and effort, so much of all that happens to us is chance, that's all, just chance.

"Who are you?" I asked him.

"But it will never matter to you who I am," he said. "In the morning you won't remember anyhow."

"But you probably saved my life."

"A lot of people 'probably' saved your life," he said. "So what?"

I must have fallen asleep because when I sat up again there was a huge bright sunny day beaming at me like a joke I hadn't heard, just the waiting, smiling Cheshire response from a world that had told it. Everything was clean and white-washed, a bright flat glow of sand and sea with a gray-blue morning sky and gulls and sandpipers and the sound of the waves, gone farther out away from us and whispering.

"Who are you?" I said to him, sleeping next to me in the sand.

"Does it really matter who I am?"

"No, not really."

He pulled me down and we made love in that early morning on the beach with a brand-new day that was smiling.

"Where were you?" the archer man asked me. "Where did you go?"

"The beach. Only the beach."

"Who were you with?"

"No one, I was only with the child."

"Why didn't you tell me where you were going? Why did you just take off like that without a word, no explanation? You knew the one thing I couldn't take was being left, being abandoned, looking for you but you weren't there. You knew it and you did it anyhow. Why did you ruin everything by leaving like that? Why couldn't you just live, just plain live with things the way they were? Why did you have to run? I can't trust you now or ever again."

That's what he said to me, old swan, mean, ugly, rotten stinking swan. But it's just as well, he had a lot of problems, he wasn't perfect, but I loved him. That's the funny part, I think I really loved him. I didn't tell him I was pregnant then. I let him go and never said a word to him about the baby. Why, you ask. Because I didn't want to share it with him, I didn't want to hold him that way after what he said to me, I didn't want to tell, that's all, I didn't want to tell him because if I had, he would have stayed with me, he would have always stayed with me if he knew, and for some reason, that frightened me.

Though I know that evening's empire
Has returned into sand,
Vanished from my hand,
Left me blindly here to stand but still not sleeping.
My weariness amazes me
I'm branded on my feet.
I have no one to meet
And the ancient empty street's too dead for dreaming.

Hey, Mr. Tambourine man, play a song for me
In the jingle jangle morning, I'll come following you.

Did I tell you, swan, I got a card from the Turtle. He said he's coming home.

14

How long have I been asleep? How long have we been traveling? When will we be home? The train is chugging softly in the night, the Turtle is sleeping, his chin is resting on his shirt, his mouth is open. The great huge Turtle man is resting loose and going soft in sleep. His shoes are spotless, his suitcase contained behind him, nice and square and gray with luggage tags and a plastic place for an address card, locks and a combination, just exactly what the Turtle longed for, a suitcase with a combination lock.

"Look, Turtle, you've got to get up. I have a few things to talk to you about."

"Sure," he says and sits up with a start, "sure, what is it?"

"I'm pregnant, that's what it is. I'm going to have a baby. You've been away a long time, it was the anniversary of the child's death. I tried to tell you but you wouldn't hear. There was this man, the golden archer man. I wanted a child, Turtle, nothing personal, nothing to get all upset about. I simply needed to be full again. I needed it an awful lot. I tried to tell it all to you, but you went away, you didn't hear me, you couldn't listen anymore. You didn't understand about the car, I tried to tell you I needed, Turtle, but you didn't believe in needing, you don't think it happens, but it does."

"Did anyone ever tell you," the Turtle begins, "that you're all fucked up, you're all fucked up and I'm tired of it. I went away because I was tired of how all fucked up you were. I couldn't hear you anymore and I didn't understand and so I thought it would be better if I got away from you and tried to think a little, but you can't think when you love someone, you can't figure things out, you just love them. I loved you. There was never another woman in my life, not before you, not since you. I never looked at other women, I never saw them, I never cared. You were beautiful to me and soft and lost and helpless. I thought I could help you. I thought I could rescue the helpless child you were. I thought I could fill up all the loneliness and heartache. I thought I could make it all up to you. I thought I could keep you solid and together, that you could empty yourself to me, could clean it all out and start over, and I thought I could give because I loved you so much. Night and day I loved you and I put myself right there for you. But I wasn't your brother and I wasn't flashy, I wasn't all fucked up enough for you, and love wasn't enough. Why wasn't love enough? It's supposed to be.

"The car, the car, all I've heard about has been the car, not the child, just the car, but the car was something like not returning a library book to the public library. Nothing malicious, nothing rotten and evil, an oversight while my mind was crammed with four thousand different things going on, work and money, how to keep a family together, pay the bills with a wife who was nuts. Every other word was about your brother for twelve long, long, hard and heartbreaking years, but your face was pretty and you clung to me in bed at night and you made love with me and it was marvelous, the way you needed it, the way you wouldn't compromise about that, just that, and I stayed and I hoped and I tried. I brought you priests and Bibles and I helped you get the things you needed when you got sick, when you broke in half and you were scattered on the floor like a china vase, I swept the pieces up and put them in the laundry bag and took them to the first doctor and the second and twentieth until they carted you away all shattered even more, clutching a paintbrush and talking to formless creatures calling you in the night. They took you away from me and I was left alone without you, without you clinging in the night. I slept in your studio, do you know? I slept and cried with the children in your studio. There were two then, a boy and a girl, a boy you called your brother's son. 'He looks so like my brother, doesn't he?' But you never saw him, never reached for him for a minute of his life. He never looked a thing like your brother, did you know? Could you ever know he looked nothing like your brother? But you wouldn't hear a word of that. And the little girl, our little girl, I never said a word to you except you did your best. What in God's name did you want? What in God's name could anyone give you that you didn't take and find it wasn't what you wanted anyhow? But how you clung in the dark all night long. Yes, I went away because if I had stayed I would have lost my sense, my mind, the things that keep a man together. I had to go away but I came back like I said I would. I went away and cried and walked and cried and I came back because there are no decisions. I loved you. All the rest of it isn't what makes the difference, all the heartache doesn't ruin it, love is a lot of things, did you know that? It's need and I needed you and I thought you needed me.

"Infidelity is a beggar, an impoverished hungry beggar. I tried to make it all up for you but no one can. Didn't you ever find out that the only thing that matters in the whole of living is the deal you make with one other person, the waiting and the trying and the pitching in, didn't anyone ever tell you that? Why was it always your brother? For him the door was always open.

"Who were you fucking around with while I was away? Couldn't wait a couple of weeks. That's all it was, baby, seven or eight weeks. Couldn't wait, could you? Did it start the very next day, or the night before I left? When did it start, baby? Was it going on for years or is it still brand-new and beautiful? Who is he, what did he look like, what could he give you? You're all fucked up, baby, all out of whack, done.

"I know, I'll tell you," the Turtle says, he's lighting a cigarette, the night train speeding onward home. "I'll tell you. He's blond and thin, his face is high ruddy red, his eyes are blue, he is quick and glib, an intellect, fancy ideas, someone who is going to change the world out there, a kid, a dreamer who can't make his own small spot happen but the big world out there, that's different, that he can manage, and maybe he can, but it's not going to matter, it's not going to make you happy, but I don't really care anymore.

"I lost a child too, did that ever occur to you? No, only this new one who is a ringer for your brother's face, but it's an illusion, it's a dream. Did you know it's all a dream? You don't understand you can't go home, you can't go backwards without losing everything—didn't you know that? All your little boys with blond hair and blue eyes drifting in and out of my life. I've seen them all, I've waited for them all to go home but they never did. I pulled you twice from the window, screaming 'Come and walk with me, walk it off with me, does it run in families?' I pulled you by the hair back into life and it's taken all I have, I don't have anything, not anymore. People think they can change someone else just because they want to, just because they love that other person, just because they've made a deal with themselves to make it, to really make it for another human being and for themselves. But the secret is, that other human being needs something no one can give him. They need a dream to be broken over and over again, they need to be destroyed and reconstructed just so they can be destroyed again and that's their whole sad hopeless little lousy story and they take you with them. When the street was talking to you, begging you to jump into her and end, you decided to do it another way, not bravely, not all at once, but instead to do it slowly over a long time and take a lot of other people with you, isn't that so? If you're all fucked up, you stay that way, no matter how much help and love and time you get, you stay that way, no matter what anyone tells you, you stay that way.

"Why don't you go and live with this brand-new man, the father of your child? I'll let you go, I'm going myself. I'm done, and if he gets tired of it in a while, then you can always go to your brother. Isn't that really what you want to do, deep down in there, isn't that where you feel you belong? You've never let go, you cling to ghosts, baby, things long since done."

"The whole world is incest, Turtle man," I said to him, "the whole big, lousy, dirty, fucking world is incest. Universal incest, universal clinging, universal struggling for liberation, and what it costs is suffering and universal loss. How does it feel to stand alone at the top of the world, Turtle man, does the wind hurt you when it hits you in the face?"

And in the shifting compartment light, the sleeping face is handsome as it comes alive. "Don't leave me, Turtle, I can't make it without you, I'll change, I'll completely change, forgive me, Turtle, forgive and help me, I need you for everything. The handsome Turtle steady man who knew how to love and stay and keep constant and give, don't go away, old Turtle love, don't leave me, I can't make it without you. The kind Turtle who makes people grow and hear and see, gentle and steady, an all-right, good, strong Turtle man, don't go away, or else I'll be destroyed." Another hour till we're home, I'll work on him, I'll do a job on him, I'll make him change. The train is slowing down to stop somewhere, God knows where.

"Turtle love," I say to him—but he is grabbing the things he has and getting off, somewhere in the night far away from anyplace we've ever seen before; the Turtle's going.

"What have I done to deserve this?" I wring my hands at him. "She's dead, you're leaving me like this, tell me in

God's name what have I done, Turtle. I'll change, please, I'll be good and I'll stay tight, don't leave, don't go away. When will you be back? Are you coming back? I thought I could be honest with you. I thought we could have a real exchange, truth between two people can be possible."

"Honesty is as worthless as lies," the Turtle says. "Truth is something else and our truth isn't anymore."

The shiny shoes and suitcase with the combination lock are leaving and with them, all things real.

"Hey Turtle, it's Sunday, we're getting married today, don't you remember, we're going to get married today, Turtle, how do you like that? Wake up, Turtle," I said to him, "we're going to get married."

He was a shy Turtle man, quiet and almost ready to smile. "Yeah," he said, "five more minutes, just let me sleep for five more minutes."

"Hey Turtle," I said, "do you remember when you were a kid and you'd yell out the window of a car at passing strangers, 'Hello, how are you,' you would shout and they would smile at you and you'd almost burst from finding that the world was full of smiling friendly people who would smile back at you. It was wonderful, do you remember, Turtle?"

"Yes," he said, "five more minutes, come on, just five more minutes, we'll be married for a long time, just give me five more minutes."

"I feel like that today, Turtle love, I feel like that today, I'm happy, Turtle."

"Everything is going to be all right," he groaned up at me from the pillow, he threw an arm over me and pulled me down and kissed my head and said everything is going to be all right.

"Hey, Turtle," I said, "it's snowing out, all the whole wide world is white because we are getting married today, what do you think, old Turtle love?" and he was sleeping smiling.

"I'm going to teach you everything I know, old Turtle love, I'm going to show you how the birds learn how to fly, I'll even show you flying birdhouses that set somewhere behind the sun, I'll show you how to draw them, flying over there behind the sea, we'll watch them and we'll learn and you'll understand it all. I want you to understand it all the way I do, I want you to hear the notes I can hit and maybe someday you can hit them too, and I can do it all for you, I know I can do it all for you, I have to do it all for you, it's my destiny. I'm going to make you happy, Turtle man, the meaning of my life is to make you happy." He smiled at me again, not sure, never sure if it would ever really happen, if he could ever really understand at all what happy was. He looked at me as if to say, Please, please, if you can't, no one ever will.

I tugged the Turtle to the foot of the great mountain. He was afraid but he came that far with me. "Up there," I said, "is where we have to go. Somehow we have to get up there where the air is clean and all around for as far as you can see there is beauty and peace and understanding. Up there there are no limits, Turtle love, up there is only the infinite possibility of freedom. Up there is where we have to go, are you ready?"

"Yes," he said, he hoped that he was ready, he trusted me then and so he thought that he might be ready. "First we have to throw the dishes out the window of the boat, then a shoe, and then a belt. It won't hurt. It's a simple exercise in throwing things away, nothing can accumulate until tomorrow, life is happening right now and things are only worth the fun they bring. First I'll throw, then you, then me, then you. Are you ready, Turtle man?"

"Yes," he said, and belched, and then he started laughing nervous jerky laughs and the dishes went and the shoes and the belt. "It's wrong to do this."

"No," I told him, "it's not wrong, it's essential. First me, then you, then me, then you, it's only a beginning exercise.

"Hey, Turtle, what do you think? The beach slopes down to the sea in the last golden hours of the day and we can watch it here quiet beside the sea. Come sit with me and tell me what you're thinking. I feel the warm mist holding me sitting next to you. What are you thinking, Turtle man? I love you very much."

He smiled at me, still waiting for something to begin, and I held his hand. Please, please, his eyes said to me, if you can't no one ever will, and I thought I could then, I thought I really could.

The moon was over the ocean. We slept out on the beach and watched the moon-silver nights close to each other, with the warm air like a blanket over us, and we drew the birds in flight and we heard each other trying and we were very happy. The child brought tears to the Turtle's eyes. He held the child and the tears were always in his eyes, and when he looked at me there was something misty all over him. He glowed then when he looked at me and I thought there were endless things still to happen for the Turtle and for me, still a whole lot of new world that I could give him and I still thought he wanted it from me.

Hey, Turtle, why didn't you stay? Why did you leave? What went wrong? If you come back I'll tell you all about how I went to the hospital all alone and had it taken care of, about the child. It was a little room and I waited there. Another girl was in the other bed. We didn't talk to each other. She had her husband with her. They took her up fifteen minutes before they took me and when they brought me back I wasn't pregnant anymore, all done. A little air machine, they told me, sucked the child still alive right out of me. "Turn on more air," the doctor said he told the nurse up there, "more air." Get the little seed, the little cashew nut all white lying in a bag of life, more air to suck it out. No more than four minutes and it was done, a lifetime done and never begun all at once, blue eyes like the great archer man, flecked with brown, red-blond hair, a boy, a girl, strong healthy

lungs, maybe a birthmark on the arm, maybe humor and
wit, maybe softness and love, maybe an evil temper—none of
it will ever be. Another loss, old Turtle man, and I'm bleed-
ing my insides out alone. It's hot, the city comes up at me
like a furnace. I came home that very day, a taxi cab, it's all
right, what's the difference, there was no funeral in the oper-
ating room, they probably flushed it down the toilet, the
archer man's child, and then they let me sleep it off till four.
A male nurse came and walked me to the street, I felt groggy,
wanted a cigarette but I didn't have one with me, too groggy
to go and buy a pack. The little boy looks a lot like you in
the lazy four o'clock. It's hot in the city, it's hot here, and I
wish that you'd come back, don't know why, there are no rea-
sons, only wish that you'd come back. This is the top of the
world, all alone, a windy tearstained face where the butterfly
is circling round and round. Try to grab him to your cheeks
and make him stay with his beauty and his song, around your
eyes and nose and scar. This is the top of the world with a
wind that comes out from so far away I can't see a horizon,
there are no horizons anymore, no measure of distance, just
timeless space along with a lot of remorse and not to fall
apart from remembering. I'm not falling apart, old Turtle
man. You'd be proud of me. I'm standing tall and not falling
apart although there isn't any reason to keep together, none
that I can see. Will someone ever come to take the things I've
kept collected in a brown paper bag? Everything I know is in
this paper bag I'm holding here. I want someone to sit close to
me beside the sea again. I want to start again from scratch
with all my scars. I've reclaimed myself from the lost-and-
found, no one came for me so I reclaimed myself. In my own
unimportance I understand a lot these days. I'm hamstrung
in the sun-baked earth for all this time until I see the golden
butterfly come winging into view. I try to press his beauty
close to my face and nose and eyes, and in trying to inhale all
his timelessness I heard the universal thing of all alone, that
was where I was, waiting for the phone to ring, waiting for

the Turtle man to come back with his shiny shoes to say it was not all that bad, that things would be all right. Remember Christmas that first year, the tree and all the little gifts with stockings filled with good real things, remember Christmas morning, Turtle man, how warm it was? I tried to make it all come true for us but I couldn't, no matter how I tried I wasn't there with you for long enough. So you couldn't hear my song after all, could you, Turtle man? Soon I left. I drifted out the windows on the snowing day away, all away, looking for another dream I couldn't name. What did you say that dream was, Turtle man? "Ghosts and things I cling to long since done." Maybe so, but we were special people, my brother and I, we were extraordinary. I'm painting well these days, though, anyhow. Swans that aren't anymore beside a stream that's all gone dry, a house up on a hill that blinked its eyes closed tight forever on a million dreams that broke my heart, and there's monumental regret for things that I can't even name. Confusion, remorse, what went wrong? I always try to find the answer, what went wrong. I really tried but it never happened right for me, I guess. Still drifting in circles that don't go anywhere.

Hey, Turtle, where did summer go? What happened to the yellow lace leaves? I could have been a good writer, but so what? Children passing by the lady in the park who draws the swan out on the pond stop and look and laugh behind their hands at her. They don't understand at first the strange yellow swans and so they laugh at the funny lady painting there who wears a funny hat and dress and stops what she is doing to watch them laugh at her behind their hands—why are they laughing, Turtle man? Waiting for the phone to ring to say you were just away but you'll be coming back. The child asks me where you are. Away, I tell him, but you'll be back. I've grown bizarre and strange with chiffon scarves and full-brimmed hats and a velvet band around my neck, no shoes, waiting for the phone to ring saying you're coming back. Will you be coming back? I can't believe you would abandon me without a word, without a card, without a line, no signature. Why didn't I ever live what I had, why were the dreams always better than the things I had? It's hot, I don't know where to put myself at night. Hey, Turtle, today my brother called. I didn't have a chance to speak with him. I didn't want to speak with him, I guess, I'm not quite certain what I want. He asked me to come out and stay a while with him. I didn't answer him, said I'd call him back but I haven't yet. He sends me pictures of the house he built that overlooks the sea, little words all scribbled in the side, but I haven't called him back. The boy wants to come and live with you. I think he should if you'll agree, there isn't much that I can do for him, not anymore.

Too bad, isn't it, the way things went for us, a lot of dreams, an awful lot of dreams we almost made, we should have made them, Turtle man, why didn't we? So many times I see you standing in the hall, right over there, telling me that everything will be all right. What will be all right, old Turtle man? I couldn't help it, the way I slopped through life hobbling, distorted. I always said I did my best, but I didn't, did you always know I didn't even try, I didn't know where to begin.

What was the boredom that made me border madness all the time, shaking my leg and tearing the bits of paper up, tapping my fingers all the time, whistling and looking around, what was I looking for, what was I always looking for—where will I ever find it? The archer man? No, he was just another pair of shoes. For a little while he was more, but then he became just another pair of shoes. All I ever really like in life is cock and chocolate pudding—not very admirable, but absolutely true. If I could have had enough of either all the time, I'd be all right. Did I tell you that my brother called? "Come on out," he said—"a house that overlooks the sea and at night the color is rose gold coming in with fog and foghorns that sound like great tired birds that soothe." He said there's a room for me where I can paint the whole damn

day away, a piano and a cat and all the dresses I can wear—
"Come on," he said, "we'll have a ball for as long as you
want the ball to last. You can have a gigolo," he said "and I
can have some chicks and if not, we'll work. All over the
world we'll work." Oh Turtle, you never understood what
it's like to make something happen with your flying hands
and storming mind splashing out across an untouched stretch
of virgin white. To create. All the people that he runs with
these days are crazy full of talent, they wouldn't laugh at me
behind their hands, they wouldn't give me a priest when I
needed a swan. It's no one's fault really, the different way
that people are, no one to blame, it's just the way it is. "But
what about the Turtle?" I said to him, "he might be coming
back and if he's coming back, I have to wait." My brother
said you won't be coming back, he said I fucked it up. "I
liked him though," my brother said, "I never knew how
much I really liked the Turtle till he left."

Oh Turtle man, do you remember Portugal that year, it
was hot, must have been one hundred and five but there was
a breeze. I never could stand the heat but the breeze made it
all okay, could never stand hot rooms either. Do you remember all the little tile houses tucked up in front of the sea, the
women wearing black out on the beaches lining up the fish
the boats brought in at dusk, the crazy rows of fish out on the
beach and how we ate sardines and walked through the little
twisting funny streets that ran on like an aging caterpillar all
full of little shops and people watching us, holding hands
and eating and laughing with our mouths full? You bought a
rose for me and put it in my hair and they thought that I was
native. The sea went out at night around the huge enormous
rocks where we sat drinking wine and making love behind
the rocks on the beach by the sea. You loved me then, I think
you really loved me, and I was happy, I was free, those
nights, walking on the beach, talking, it was wonderful.

Hey, Turtle, where did summer go? I'm painting well
these days. You're the only man I ever loved. I really wanted

you but you were never there, someplace else, always some-place else even when you were there, you were always some-place else or else you were asleep—anyhow, my brother called.

I think I'll go with him awhile. I sort of have to, don't know why but that it seems real for me somehow. I'm really painting well these days, I think if that's all that I will ever make in life, then I'll make it good, if it's really all that I can do, then I'm really going to do it—what I can.

He said he'd buy me all the dresses I can wear, silk shawls from China with a mile of fringe and, Turtle, all the choco-late pudding I can eat. I'm going to bring a swan to him, a little baby swan, he'll like that, a big surprise—I can see his face, "Oh my God," he'll say, "a baby swan." And he'll shake his head a little bit and look all wistful. You see, the things I bring to him won't be mistakes, won't be the wrong size, won't be burdens. I always ran to get you things you couldn't use, you never wanted them, me running with these things, thinking they were marvelous. But you didn't, you never thought they were marvelous. But they were me and you didn't understand it, not at all. He does, he always under-stands. Ah, Turtle, no one's fault, there is no blame.

It's autumn now, the leaves are all in bloom giving their last burst, their last valiant splurge before the chill. Great paper flowers blooming out across a cardboard fence and soon the rains will start, the wind will drive the falling leaves, the world will turn a copper brown and I don't want to be alone. When I'm with him I'm not alone, all the rest of the time with all the rest of the people, somehow I am. It doesn't mat-ter who I'm with, I'm still alone and I look for him no mat-ter where I am, I look for him. Something about comfortable shoes, something about loose-fitting clothes that don't con-strict, something about being warm and right inside, some-thing not foreign, something real. That's what it really is. We're not a burden to each other. Turtle man, we laugh, we make fun of things, ugly people, boring people, we make

such fun of them and laugh. He makes me laugh so hard
sometimes I think it's really dangerous. I can't catch my
breath with the tears streaming down my face, the way he
makes me laugh. You used to make me laugh like that a little
bit, but it's always like that with him, he's funny, my God
he's funny. The action is always where he is, he draws it in
with his exuberance, he's alive and has a million dreams and
plans he hasn't even scratched yet. When I'm with him it's
not a chore to breathe.

We never lost each other, we were never away from each
other no matter where we were, no matter who we were with,
we were with each other. Such talented children, that's what
they used to say about us. Mother always said all we needed
was each other. She used to talk about "superior people." She
made it hard for us, talking that way. I think she almost
made us believe it.

Anyhow, the children in the park won't laugh at me behind their hands, not where we will be. He said he'll write
a Christmas play, the way he did when we were young, remember? Do you remember? He said he feels it all coming
back to him again. He said there will be a room for me that's
filled with sun gold where I can paint the whole damn day
away, he built a house that's on a hill that overlooks the sea, a
piano and a cat, can you imagine, Turtle man, a piano and a
cat.

About the Author

Fredrica Wagman lives in Philadelphia with her husband and four children. She is at work on her second novel.